SPECIAL MESSAGE TO READERS

THE ULVERSCROFT FOUNDATION
(registered UK charity number 264873)
was established in 1972 to provide funds for research, diagnosis and treatment of eye diseases.
Examples of major projects funded by the Ulverscroft Foundation are:-

- The Children's Eye Unit at Moorfields Eye Hospital, London
- The Ulverscroft Children's Eye Unit at Great Ormond Street Hospital for Sick Children
- Funding research into eye diseases and treatment at the Department of Ophthalmology, University of Leicester
- The Ulverscroft Vision Research Group, Institute of Child Health
- Twin operating theatres at the Western Ophthalmic Hospital, London
- The Chair of Ophthalmology at the Royal Australian College of Ophthalmologists

You can help further the work of the Foundation by making a donation or leaving a legacy.
Every contribution is gratefully received. If you would like to help support the Foundation or require further information, please contact:

THE ULVERSCROFT FOUNDATION
The Green, Bradgate Road, Anstey
Leicester LE7 7FU, England
Tel: (0116) 236 4325
website: www.foundation.ulverscroft.com

THE MODEL MURDERS

When Mornia Garish's body was found dead, she became the fifth such victim in two years. The police believed the crimes were the work of a maniac. Then another sinister pattern emerged: they had all recently posed nude for portraits by the artist Gilbert Reeves. Determined to escape from her poor background, Rebecca Kay takes all manner of risks to become a top-line model. But when she agrees to pose for Reeves, has she taken a risk too far?

NORMAN FIRTH

THE MODEL MURDERS

Complete and Unabridged

LINFORD
Leicester

First published in Great Britain

First Linford Edition
published 2015

A catalogue record for this book is available
from the British Library.

ISBN 978–1–4448–2267–0

Published by
F. A. Thorpe (Publishing)
Anstey, Leicestershire

Set by Words & Graphics Ltd.
Anstey, Leicestershire
Printed and bound in Great Britain by
T. J. International Ltd., Padstow, Cornwall

This book is printed on acid-free paper

1

Model Wanted

Working girl wanted as model by professional photographer. Must not be averse to posing for undraped studies of the female form. No professional models need apply. Box 1428.

That was what the advert said. And that was the start of the most adventuresome and colored part of my life.

I was eighteen when I saw it, and working in a sweatshop off Miniver Street in Brooklyn. The sweatshop was run by a man named Blackthorn, and you can bet we had a better name than that for him when we spoke amongst ourselves. I'd worked there ever since I'd left school at fourteen; jobs were hard to get, and I didn't have any special talents, apart from reasonable looks and a nice shape.

My father and mother were hard-working Brooklyn people, according to my *father*. Actually, myself and mother did all the work and brought home the money which paid for father's drinks and smokes. All father *ever* did was amble along to the pool hall every day and lounge around losing our money. He'd come home about six and say he'd been looking for work all day; then he'd eat and go out again.

Mother never dared to question him: she simply accepted her hard luck in having married him and went right on working for him and my two younger sisters.

My own life was the drabbest thing you could imagine. I never had enough money to buy the clothes I wanted and to have my hair done in a decent style. All I could ever afford was a dollar to have the ends curled down at Sal's on the corner. I had to use cheap make-up, and I had to wipe it off before father came in or he wouldn't have been above tanning me with his belt, as old as I was. Nor dare I smoke in front of him, or let slip the fact that I went dancing occasionally with the nice boy from the next floor of the tenement we lived in.

I was lucky if I could scrape together a few paltry cents to go to the movies once a week, or have a Coke down at the drugstore. But Billy — the only boyfriend I bothered with — used to take me dancing and to the latest movies, and that was what made me so restless and dissatisfied. None of the other girls at the sweatshop seemed to have any ambition. They seemed to take their low station in life for granted, never wanted to have things, to do things, to go places. If I ever mentioned to them that someday I'd get somewhere I used to get laughed down.

And then that day when I saw that newspaper ad., I knew my chance had arrived!

Why a professional photographer should want a working girl for a model I didn't quite understand. I was too innocent then to read into it the implications older girls would have, but I did feel that it would mean a new life and a new way of living for me, if I could be lucky enough to get the job. So I determined to try.

I said nothing to anybody for the moment. I wrote the Box Number that same night a short letter in my neatest hand:

The Advertiser,
Box 1428,
The Daily Clarion.
Dear Sir,

In answer to your advertisement in the *Clarion*, I am making my application for the position you offer. I am eighteen, tall, and am considered good-looking. I am at present working at Blackthorn's, Miniver Street, Brooklyn, but would be able to secure time off for an interview when suitable to you.

Hoping you will give my application your favorable consideration,

REBECCA KAY

Reading it over it seemed terrible. It was stilted and had no personality. It was just such a letter as a hundred other girls would be sure to write with the aid of their little book on letter-writing. A text-book letter. So I tore it up and decided I couldn't lose anything by trying another method. If the advertiser had any human instincts surely I could write something which would excite pity, amusement, curiosity and, perhaps, a faint admiration and desire to see the writer?

My second attempt was audacious.

Dear Sir,

I spotted your ad. in the *Clarion*. It seems to be just the chance I've waited for to get out of the stinking sweatshop I work in. And *work is right!*

In fact, it seems to me you can be a stepping stone for me to attain better things — you give me the start and I feel sure my determination and passable looks and figure will do the rest.

How about it? Mind if I step in on you?

If you will set a time for an interview I'll see if I can make it.

Yours sincerely,
REBECCA KAY

And though I was half afraid he'd throw the letter away as a piece of downright impertinence, I sent it that night,

5

and spent the following two days in a dither, until at last I gave it up, feeling certain he must have found a model elsewhere.

But the third morning there was a letter in the post for me!

Luckily father never came from bed until after nine, and I was alone when I opened it. What he would have said if he'd had any idea that I meant to pose for a man, and undraped at that, I couldn't begin to imagine. Probably he'd have done his talking with the buckle end of his belt.

The letter said:

Dear Miss Kay,

If you care to call on me at my studio on 44th Street, I will be pleased to see you. There is no necessity to arrange a set time. Come after you have finished work for the day — you'll find me in.

Yours faithfully,
MICHAEL PATTERSON

I pushed the letter down the top of my stocking with trembling fingers. I did that because, if I put it in my bag, father might go through it at dinnertime looking for odd cents, as he very often did. Then I hurried off to work, full of excitement.

I told Mary, one of the girls who had always been a firm friend of mine. She was almost as excited as I was myself, and read the letter with envy and wide eyes.

'Gee, kid, it sure looks good to me. And say, what a Ritzy address . . . but you want to make sure this guy isn't just a bum and a wolf. You know the kind, and you'd be fair game for a heel like that. But if it *is* on the level . . . '

'I feel certain it is Mary,' I replied. 'Something tells me it's straight enough.'

'Sure you wouldn't like me to trip along with you so's I can keep an eye on the guy?'

'No thanks, Mary. He might think that was funny, mightn't he? I'll go alone — I don't think there'll be any trouble about it.'

The day passed all too slowly. I think the other girls knew I was all worked up about something, and they looked at me curiously and asked questions. But I didn't want to say anything then, for if

I didn't get the job I knew how skitty they could be. I just laughed their enquiries off and went on with my job.

At dinnertime father was out, but mother noticed my nervous tension. She said: 'Becky, what's the matter with you? You're all of a bounce today. Is something wrong?'

'Nothing, mother — only that — I think I'm going to have a better job soon. At least, I hope so. I can't tell you now, but if I'm lucky I will. I'll need you to help square father.'

She didn't ask me anything more; she trusted me.

During the afternoon the hammer and hum of the sewing machines got well and truly on my nerves. I messed up three pairs of union pants in my impatience, and was well and truly told off by the thin-lipped supervisor. But at last the afternoon came to an end, and at six o'clock we streamed out into the street. I caught a street car for the river.

I was a bit nervous about knocking at the door of the office I eventually arrived at. On it, in gilt lettering, were the words:

8

Michael J. Patterson, Starlight Studio.

It was on the top floor and was a studio apartment, as I could see when I got inside. A trim, blonde secretary admitted me and said Mr. Patterson would not be a moment, would I sit down? I sat down beside three other girls, who all seemed to be from working-class families, and who were just as nervous as I was.

The door to the inner room opened and a red-haired girl came out. She was a little red about the cheeks, and it wasn't an over-application of rouge. She hurried right out without speaking to anyone, and then a young man appeared at the door of the studio itself and said:

'Next please.'

One of the other girls went inside, and whilst I waited I had a chance to weigh up my feelings about the young man. He was not more than twenty-eight, with fair wavy hair, and a keen look about him. Not really good-looking, but good-natured looking, with a firm set to his jaws, and a high square forehead. His clothing consisted of a shabby and shiny pair of flannel trousers, and a much-worn green sports jacket. I began to feel a little better about my own somewhat worn clothes.

The girl came out; he was saying: 'Thank you, Miss Green. I will inform you of my decision in a few days' time. Good night.'

One by one the remaining girls went in, stayed for about ten minutes, and came out again. Finally only I remained. He looked at me, then said: 'Miss . . . ?'

'Kay, sir. Rebecca Kay.'

'Oh, of course,' he said, giving me a charming smile. 'The young lady who is very keen on using me as a stepping stone. Come in, Miss Kay.'

I grabbed nervously at my bag and went in. It was a big studio, with a lot of photographic equipment all about, and three or four large cameras. There were three large open skylights, and all of one wall was a sheet of glass. The evening sun streamed into the studio, spreading a golden tint over the nude cabinet portraits on the wall, and over the chaise-longue, which was covered by a heavily embroidered cloth.

10

He indicated the faded armchair before the small desk, and said:

'Please sit down. Miss Kay. I have your letter here.'

I stammered: 'I hope you don't think it was awfully cheeky of me, Mister Patterson . . .'

'Oh, but I do. I certainly do. So I'm to be your stepping stone, young woman, am I?'

But he was grinning at the letter whilst he was speaking, and it wasn't a derisive grin. He stood up and looked me up and down, then said: 'I've had an extremely harassed day, Miss Kay. Look at me — I'm worn out. I've interviewed girls of all shapes and sizes. Some remarkable shapes, and some most peculiar sizes. One young lady who wrote and mentioned that she was really elegant, slim and well formed, turned out to weigh just under two tons, and to be about as elegant as a garbage collector. Well — ' he smiled — 'perhaps not *quite* two tons . . . but she was certainly more than twelve stones. You'd be surprised, Miss Kay, to learn that out of thirty-four girls I

11

have seen, only two came anywhere being near suitable for models. And one of those seemed to imagine I wanted her to do her posing in a bedroom, and the other had apparently overlooked the portion of the ad. which stated I needed a girl who would be able to pose undraped. At any rate, she walked out when I suggested she strike a pose . . . if you are of the same turn of mind, Miss Kay . . . ?'

'Why — er — no, of course not,' I stuttered. 'I — er — I understand that it's part of your business, of course.' I flushed just the same, and a little amused quirk covered the corners of his lips. He said:

'And you would have no objections to nude photographs of yourself appearing in the popular magazines?'

'None — no . . . I . . . I don't think so.'

'You don't *think* so?' he raised his eyebrows. 'Don't you *know*? Would you have objections?'

'Yes . . . that is, I mean . . . no. None.'

He looked me over again, carefully. But there was nothing in his eyes but pure criticism. At last he murmured: 'Your face is all right — and your height. You should prove photogenic. We'll see.' He nodded to a screen in the corner, said: 'Would you slip out of your things behind there? We'll take a quickie and see how it comes out.'

He busied himself with his camera. I hesitated, red in the face.

'Well?' he said in surprise.

'I — I mean — *everything*?'

'Naturally. You'll find a dressing gown behind the screen. You can slip it on until I'm ready for you.'

I went back of the screen.

I undressed slowly, and noticed that my hands were trembling and my legs knocking together. My body burned with fright and shame, and I wanted to put my clothes on again and run from the studio. I would have done so had I not been afraid of showing myself to be a little fool. For that was all I was . . . there was nothing nasty about it at all, except in my mind. And as I slipped into the dressing robe, a bit of courage returned to me, and I called: 'Ready.'

I went out, and he didn't even look up. He was still fussing with his camera, fitting a plate. He began to talk, however.

I expect he had an idea how a girl who was unused to posing this way would feel about it, and he wanted to ease my mind.

'Won't be a minute — I suppose this is the first time you've posed in your life for a professional photographer, eh?'

'I — I once posed for a beach photographer at Coney Island,' I murmured sheepishly.

'I'd hardly call him a professional,' he chuckled. 'But you mustn't be embarrassed by this — ordeal, shall we say? The feminine body is a thing of joy and beauty forever, especially the young undraped form. Looked at from the purely impersonal eye of art there is nothing suggestive about it. Do you yourself not agree that the portraits you see about these walls are very far removed from anything earthy? Don't you think they are things of grace and beauty? Not only to men, but to anyone?'

I looked at them, murmured: 'I — I really can't say.'

He was finished with the camera at last, and he lowered a long roll of black velvet opposite the big window. Then he set a small pedestal before it, threw a white rope over the rafter above it, formed a noose at the lower end, and tested it with his hand.

'We'll not take long to get this over with,' he told me, measuring distances with a tape and studying angles. He went to the window again, lowered two blinds on the right, then covered up one of the skylights. Again he studied the pedestal and the black cloth. He said: 'That'll do — now just slip out of the robe and put your head in that noose, will you, Miss Kay?'

I almost fainted!

2

The Bet

He waited for me to do as he asked. I said: 'Put — put my head in the — noose?'

'Exactly. Stand on the pedestal before the velvet and put your head in the noose.'

'But . . . '

'As if you were hanging,' he explained. 'It'll be unusual. I'll call it Farewell, after the song. Or maybe I'll call it despair, or betrayal, or simply 'The Attic.' You see? Think of the possible constructions that can be placed on the portrait of a naked woman hanging in shadows. It gives food for *thought* — and that's what I like my studies to give.'

I was floored. I went over and got on the pedestal. I let the gown slide down from my rounded figure with a silent prayer. He said: 'Here, before you take a pose dab your face and figure with this.' He threw me a large powder puff and brought over a box of scented white powder. He said: 'It'll give the effect I want against the black background. Go ahead.'

I dabbed myself all over with the stuff and returned the puff to him. He said: 'Strike a pose and let's see if you're any good at construing my thoughts.'

I struck a pose which I considered typical of despair. He grinned and said: 'You aren't acting in silent movies. You don't need to screw your face up into a tragic mask. Just register utter hopelessness in a sophisticated way. A blank, lifeless look, a staring of the eyes as if you look at something you can never hope to have. You get it . . . ?'

I thought of a mink coat and put the noose round my neck. He said: 'That's great. Great. Now slump until the rope is taut. Let your hands dangle by your side in a lifeless way. Tilt your head further to the right so I can get the face and the expression. Let your legs relax — drop that stiffness about the stomach.'

17

I followed his directions breathlessly. He seemed satisfied. He said: 'Okay, that's the pose. You can snap out of it now.'

I heaved a sigh of relief and said: 'That was quick.'

'What do you mean, quick? The photo isn't taken. I was just getting the right light. I'll use an arc on the left side of the camera . . . that'll throw your face into relief and your back will merge with the shadows.'

Then he found a small stool, which he raised and lowered with the turn of a handle. He adjusted this so that when I stood on it I had to stand on tiptoe to prevent myself being choked by the noose. He said: 'When the shot's taken the black stool will not show in the finished print. It'll look as if you are hanging.'

I was so interested I'd forgotten I wasn't wearing a thing. He hadn't even noticed it I don't think.

He nodded me back to the stool and measured again. Then he set his camera stand and took the shot.

'Okay, you can dismount now,' he

smiled. 'Get back into your clothes. I'll do some rushes of these.'

He left the room and I almost jumped back into my things. He was gone almost twenty minutes, but when he came back he held a wet, glossy print between thumb and forefinger, laid it down upon a tiny table, and invited me over.

'It's wonderful!' I gasped, looking at myself with awe. 'I had no idea you could make me look so—so—'

'Ethereal?' he suggested. 'I didn't. You did that yourself. The expression is perfect — what did you think of?'

'I thought of something I was never likely to have, as you told me,' I replied. 'A mink coat.'

'Good Lord! What would have happened if you'd thought of a couple of dozen pairs of nylons?' he grinned.

He laid the print aside and said: 'Miss Kay, I'm fully satisfied with you. You take well, and that print won't need any retouching. The job's yours if you want it . . . it pays thirty dollars a week, and for that you're on call anytime I need you here, which will be about two hours a day, more or less.'

I jumped with both feet: 'Oh, I'll take it, Mister Patterson. Thank you — thank you so much.'

He said: 'You'd better work the week out at your old place, and start with me next Monday. Here's a ten dollar fee for the pose you just did . . . no, no, don't refuse it. I'll get twice that amount for the print. And here's another thirty dollars — call it an advance on future salary. With this I want you to get your hair done in a more elaborate style, and have a manicurist look your nails over. I hate to have imperfect close-ups of hands in my studies. You don't mind me speaking frankly?'

I did, of course, but I didn't say so. I was on air. I said:

'Of course not. Oh, no. I'll get my hair done and — and my nails. And thank you ever so much . . . '

He said: 'Listen, I'd better tell you just what's what. Haven't you wondered why I didn't get a professional model?'

I said: 'It isn't my affair, Mister Patterson . . . '

'Naturally, it isn't. But I'll tell you anyway, then you won't suffer from any delusions. The majority of the girls I saw today seemed to imagine my purpose was entirely wicked ... they also seemed extremely disappointed when they discovered it wasn't. The truth is, Miss Kay, that I am doing this for a bet ... '

'A — a bet?'

He nodded: 'A bet between my original professional model and myself. I admit I owe her a great deal — she is one of the most sought-after models in the city. She helped me along the road to fame, and I never have denied it. We're engaged, you see. But when we had a trifling argument and she turned round and said that without her help I'd be lost and would go out of business, I retaliated by saying that I could get along if I never used a skilled model again. I was rash enough to say I could take a working girl from the city, a girl without any previous experience, and make of her as good a model as any professional who ever lived. Naturally, she dared me to try — and I confess I had doubts until you turned up, Miss Kay.

That, however, is the story.'

'Then the job is — temporary? Until you've proved your point? Then you'll take back your old model and I . . . ?'

'Not at all. When I marry Marcia I'll see she gives up any ambitions she has entirely. My wife's place will be in the home, not at wild parties and gadding around modeling for other men.'

'But I thought you said there was nothing wrong about posing for an artist?' I pointed out.

'There isn't — as long as it stops short at posing. But I know Marcia, and Marcia knows I know her. That's why I wouldn't trust her to carry on with her career.'

I couldn't understand his point of view. I said: 'You must be joking? Surely, if she's so bad, you wouldn't marry her?'

He grinned: 'I could sooner do without my best camera than Marcia. You'd understand that if you could see her . . . and you most likely will. Here, have a preview.'

He opened a drawer in his desk and rooted out a glossy print.

It was a print of an undraped woman

standing against a door jamb wearing a melancholy expression and jade earrings. The clock in the room behind her said Midnight, and the caption on the back read: Watcher by the Dead.

And in the background was a shadowy coffin.

I shuddered. But in spite of the macabre trend of my new boss's studies, I could see the woman was an undeniable beauty, with a stately, classic beauty which I never tried to kid myself I possessed. Her hair was shining and black, tied in a simple coil; her body firm and supple. Her long legs and curving thighs added to her charm and grace.

Patterson said: 'Isn't she a pip?'

I nodded: 'I can understand you wanting her, at any cost.'

He said: 'Yes, she certainly gets in my hair. Anyway, you'll see her in the flesh — yards of it — if you work for me long. That's about all for now. Report on Monday morning at about eleven and we'll see about doing a Kodachrome for *Daybreak Magazine*. Goodnight, Miss Kay.'

23

And with that he led me to the door and watched me into the elevator.

Father was out again when I got home, but mother seemed very anxious. She said: 'Where have you been since work, dear?'

I told her, omitting nothing. I don't believe she thought it was quite nice to earn a living as I proposed to but she never tried to stop me doing anything on which I had set my heart. She was worried about what father might say though, and said: 'You'd better not mention this to your father, Becky. He might not let you go through with it, child. Suppose we keep it from him as long as we can?'

I agreed with her there, and started getting ready for the date I had with Billy from the apartments below us. I went down for him when I was dressed for dancing, and found he'd slipped along to the corner drugstore for hair cream. His mother, Mrs. Weinbaum, was doing the ironing for her large family, and the kids were all out playing someplace. Old Weinbaum was with my father, drinking.

24

I was so pleased at my success with the new job that I had to tell someone. I, unwisely, told Mrs. Weinbaum. It isn't that she doesn't mean well, but she can't keep anything to herself. In spite of that fact I babbled it out to her.

'I've got a new job, Mrs. W.,' I told her. 'Thirty dollars a week and no hard work.'

'My, my,' she said with a big smile. 'Iss something, thirty dollars a week, iss it nod?'

I nodded; she went on: 'Why iss that they are paying you that much, my child? Iss not at Blackthorn's? They are not paying thirty nickels a week there.'

I said: 'No. It's in town. At a studio.'

'Iss so? Filming?'

'No, not a film studio. It's an art studio — you know, a photographic place.'

'Oh! A cashier you iss being?'

'Oh, no, nothing like that. I'm a model.'

'A model?' She stopped ironing and stared at me. 'You meaning you are posing without no clothes on you? Beckya, you iss making with me the joke isn't it?'

I blushed. 'No. It's quite true, Mrs. W. What's wrong with it? It's no worse than

— than — ' I ended lamely. The fact was I couldn't think anything up that it was no worse than — at least, I knew these simple people who lived hereabouts wouldn't consider there was anything worse.

Mrs. W. went on:

'But your father, what iss he saying when you are telling him about thiss what you do? Is he not going fanatic?'

'I — I didn't tell him yet. I don't want him to know for a while. You won't say anything, will you?'

'Me?' said Mrs. Weinbaum with an injured air. 'So helping me, I am keeping it dark. But your mother, is she approving?'

'She knows I can look after myself, and she realizes this is my chance to make a better life from the one I live now. She doesn't mind at all.'

'So,' nodded Mrs. W.. 'Well, I am wishing you every success, my dear. Whatever you are doing I am knowing you will be very successful, for you are having your head fixed onto your shoulders like it was glued there. But you will be taking my advice and being so careful you wouldn't know. I am always reading in the Sunday papers about how artist's models are becoming very dead what some people they are cutting their throats and shooting them full of holes. So you are watching your step, isn't it?'

'Oh, yes, Mrs. W. I'll watch my step . . . oh, here's Billy.'

Billy Weinbaum came in at that moment with a bottle of hair cream, said: 'Hi, Toots, how's the dream thing?'

'Oh, I'm all right, Superman,' I told him.

'Swell. We'll have a regular jamboree tonight. Mugs Tate's jamming down at Lulu's, and all the groovy kids'll be there. I'll be just a minute.'

He vanished into the bedroom to smear his unruly mop of red hair down with the cheap cream he'd bought. He was a nice boy, but really didn't act his seventeen years. He was all for jitterbugging and listening to name bands like Harry James and the Dorsey Brothers, and Red Nichols. That was his entire life. He worked as a baker's delivery boy, and didn't care one way or another if he stayed a delivery boy his whole life. There wasn't any harm in Billy, and I liked him lots — liked him, and that's all.

He breezed from the bedroom again with his hair as unruly as ever, and his freckles standing out on his newly-polished red face. He said: 'Okay, dream thing, let's go cut a curious rug. Waggle your frame for the game, dame.'

'Look, Billy,' I told him. 'Do you much mind if we don't go dancing tonight?'

'We ain't going dancing, loveboat. We're goin' jiving. There's a difference, and you know it.'

'Dancing or jiving,' I said. 'It doesn't matter. I don't feel quite like it. Mind?'

'Are you haywire? Listen . . . you'll feel all right when you hear that mellow 'cello . . . '

'I won't. And either you go where I want to, or I go home.'

'Well, all right,' he said in amazement. 'But I still say you're off the groove. Where, exactly, are you going? To listen to the long underwear characters at Carnegie Hall?'

'No, I was thinking we'd have a stroll along by the river and look at the moon.'

He gulped loudly: 'The kid's gone

screwball. Ma, send for the nearest psychiatrist. No — don't bother — I'll take care of the poor kid. Okay, Lady Rebecca, let's breeze.'

He extended his arm pompously and I had to laugh. We went out, leaving Mrs. W. smiling all over her large, dark-skinned face. We took a street car to the river and got down and walked along as close to it as we could get.

There was a fine mist coming up, and I suddenly got a nostalgic feeling for something, I don't know what. It certainly wasn't for Billy. He was walking — whilst he was trying out new steps as we went — beside me, and he obviously didn't feel any nostalgia, and probably didn't know what the word meant even.

He said at last: 'Say, silent sugar doll, what's eating you? How come no go to Lulu's Jive Parlor tonight?'

I said: 'Don't use those childish expressions so much, Billy. If you must know, I think I'm getting too old for jiving — it's — well it isn't dignified. People as old as me and in my position don't do it . . . '

He whistled: 'Okay, old lady, I'll buy. What's your position? And what'll I buy you for your ninetieth birthday?'

I told him: 'I've got a new job — an important job. I'm going places, Billy. Right to the top — I'm determined.'

He grinned: 'They make you super at the sweat factory?'

'Don't be so silly. You can't go places at Blackthorn's. No one can. I've found a new job altogether. I'm going to be an artist's model, that's what!'

He laughed outright at that: 'Quit kidding yourself, sugar cake. You ain't out of pigtails as of yet. Forget your dreams and give the handsome boy on your right a tumble, huh?'

'I'm telling you the truth. I *have* got a job as an artist's model, Billy. I mean it. I got it today.'

He stopped walking, and his face was serious. He said: 'Say, does this mean you'll be leaving the district? You aren't walking right out on me, are you, cup-cake?'

I nodded: 'That's more or less it, Billy. We had fun together, but I can't go for that kind of fun anymore. I'm going to start studying at nights now . . . no more dancing.'

'You mean you don't aim to go out with a freckled face kid like I am anymore, isn't *that* it?' he said. 'Okay, who am *I* to beef? So I *am* just a kid — and I'm glad of it. I guess I'll be a kid still when I'm as old as you are — and that's only another four months away. And I'll stay that way long as I can. I like being that way. I thought you'd stay with me, but now I see you got high-falutin' ideas. Okay, Becky, it's your life. So long.'

And without asking me anything about my new job, or what I would be doing, he drove his hands in his pockets and walked moodily away along by the river.

3

Marcia Storm

I was able to tell Mary the following morning that I had got the job. And she was just as excited as if it had been her — even more excited than I was. She was bubbling over, couldn't keep it to herself for a minute. At the midmorning break she told the other girls, and made an impressive thing of it. They were mostly skeptical: one or two were frankly disgusted, others made catty by envy.

'Thirty bucks a week, eh?' said one of those I disliked, the nasty, dirty-minded type you always find in sweatshops. 'Hmm. I'd want a darn sight more than that for *my* favors . . . '

I flared up at once: 'What do you mean by *that*, Maisie?'

'It's obvious, isn't it? You, who make yourself out to be such an innocent little darling. The goody-goody girl. Huh!'

I said between my teeth, as some of the others tittered: 'Take that back, Maisie. Take it back, or I'll . . . '

'You'll *what*? You know as well as I do that it's the truth.'

I don't count myself a warlike girl, but I can't stand remarks like that. I went at her and grabbed two fistfuls of her hair, and she thumped me in the stomach. We fell over and struggled on the floor, a mass of arms and legs and overturned sandwich lunches.

I think she was getting slightly the better of me, when a sharp, prim voice interrupted, and the supervisor was standing above us: 'Get up at once, you little sluts! Get up! How dare you brawl on the premises in your lunch time?'

We got up. Maisie adopted the whining voice and the conciliatory expression which was natural to her. She was a sneak and a rat. She whimpered: 'I'm *awfully* sorry, Miss Clamp. But Rebecca Kay started it, honestly.'

Mary flashed out in my defense: 'No, she didn't, either. That sneaking scum called her . . . '

'Be silent, Miss Jones. Allow the girl herself to state what the trouble was. *Well*, Miss Kay?'

I said: 'I couldn't help starting it, Miss Clamp. Maisie said — well, I've got a new job, posing as an artist's model. Maisie tried to imply that . . . that it was something *worse* than that.'

Miss Clamp compressed her thin lips and said: 'Everyone is entitled to their own opinion. And it *does* seem a little strange, even to me, that any artist should take an unknown working girl from honest employment and use her as a *model* . . . do I make myself clear?'

I bit my lip: 'You make yourself a little too clear, Miss Clamp. I had intended to work my notice out, but in view of the opinion you hold I doubt if I'd care to. I might have known your prim and proper appearance concealed a dirty mind!'

She almost swooned: 'Get out of this place *at once*, you impertinent little harlot! Get out!'

I got out without bothering even to pick up the money owing to me. I left the girls chuckling openly, both at myself and

Miss Clamp. As I went I heard Maisie mutter: 'I bet we never see any photographs of *her* in the magazines! She's made that whole story up — she's a liar!'

I almost turned back to tackle her again, but Miss Clamp was right behind me with a stern face.

'And bear in mind, you little slut, that I'll take care you don't get another decent job in this city,' she snapped after me.

'*Decent* job?' I said. 'Huh!'

I didn't go home. Father would be in, I knew, and he'd be sure to start asking awkward questions. And I didn't want him to know anything of the job yet; if perfect strangers — or, at any rate, people who were not by any means entitled to speak — acted as Miss Clamp had, what would my own father have to say? I shuddered to think, and had a vision of him unbuckling his heavy belt and strapping me into a pitiful submissive state. He'd done that more than once, and not so long ago.

I went first to Sal's on the corner and had one of her eight dollar perms. For an extra fifty cents she manicured and painted my nails. Then I went downtown and bought a neat, inexpensive dress of a new blue shade. I also bought powder-blue strap shoes, an imitation blue flower for my hair, and a little blue handbag.

I spent the rest of the time taking in a movie, and at half-past five I went home.

Father still wasn't among those present. Mother told me he was out at the pool hall, trying to find someone to stake him to the price of a ticket for Saturday's ball game if he could. I hoped he could, because that would mean he'd be in a good mood when he came in, and we wouldn't have to endure his bearishness around the place that night.

But he didn't.

He came in fuming; my guess is that every one of his so-called pals had turned him down on that ticket, and maybe some of them had given him a talking to as well. He was looking red about the face, a sure sign he'd had one or two drinks. He didn't speak to either me or mother until he'd eaten; then he turned to her and said: 'How much is left from the housekeeping money?'

Mother said: 'Why?'

He snarled: 'Do I have to tell you *why*, blast it? I want to know, that's all.'

She said, as calmly as she could: 'There isn't enough to buy a ticket to the ball game. If that's what you mean.'

He turned to me with an oath, said: 'How about you? I suppose you'll cry poverty, too?'

'Yes, dad,' I replied meekly. 'I only get a dollar a week for myself, you know that. The rest you take on pay day.'

'And the most of it you keep,' said mother with an unusual show of spirit. He turned on her and snapped.

'If you don't keep your mouth shut I'll shut it for you. I asked how much you had left — you told me not enough to buy a ball game ticket. Okay. That's all there is to it — I don't want to hear any more. Maybe old Weinbaum'll stake me . . . '

He gave us both a final glare, jammed his hands in his pockets, and in his shirt sleeves went down to see the Weinbaums.

He was back again in about fifteen minutes, during which time mother had taken two dollars from her purse and hidden it under a vase on the mantelshelf. He came in in a far worse temper than he'd been in before, and it seemed at first Weinbaum had turned him down as well. But the reason for his mood soon became evident.

He turned on me at once: 'So you don't tell things to your father, eh? Everybody in the building knows about you but me — me you keep it quiet from! Why didn't you say you were going to *another job*? Why didn't you tell *me*?'

I gazed helplessly at mother, who said quickly: 'Leave her alone. It'll be a step up for her . . . '

'What's wrong with Blackthorn's I'd like to know? Isn't that *good enough* for her? Isn't it? The job's steady and we know the money's there every Friday. Why can't she be content like others of her class are? What do we know about this new job of hers? Old Weinbaum says it's at a photographer's studio — well, how do we know it'll last? She may be fired . . . she's no use at bookkeeping.'

I mumbled: 'It — isn't bookkeeping. I — '

'Then what is it?'

'I — I — ' I lost my nerve and blurted it out: 'It's only — only helping to develop the negatives, father.'

He grunted: 'You're getting five dollars at Blackthorn's, and an extra dollar piece rates. How much'll you get at this new job?'

'Ten dollars,' I lied. 'I get ten dollars a week.'

He rubbed his chin, mollified a little. He said: 'I see. Why didn't you tell me about the job before?'

Mother put in: 'We didn't get the chance; you wanted to do all the talking yourself.'

He nodded: 'All right. But you, Rebecca, don't forget who the money comes to — and you needn't think because you're getting ten dollars a week that you'll get any more to spend. It'll help make up for the years we've kept you and brought you up.'

I kept quiet; I wanted to tell him he hadn't lifted a hand for years and that mother had done all the work.

But I didn't dare.

Then he began to notice things. 'Where'd you get the money to have your hair done? And what's that muck you've got on your fingernails?'

Mother said: 'The firm she's going to work for advanced her a little money . . . '

'Why? Wasn't she good enough for them as she was?'

Mother sighed: 'The job's downtown. She has to look neat.'

'How much did they advance you?' he rapped at me.

'Ten dollars,' I lied.

'And how much have you left?'

'I — five dollars and a few cents.'

He smiled nastily: 'And you said you wouldn't lend me anything for a ticket, did you? Said you *hadn't* any money . . . why, I'll . . . '

He began to unbuckle his belt. For the first time in her life mother defied him. She got in front of me, said: 'Don't touch her Harry. If you lay a finger on her, so help me I'll report you! If you want the money for a ticket I expect she'll lend you two dollars . . . '

I had opened my bag and flung the five

dollars at him. I said:

'You can have it all.' I was so fed up and disgusted. He took it without another word; he looked at mother and there was murder in his eyes. He said softly: 'You've forgotten yourself, I think. You must be out of sorts. But if you ever *dare* to defy me again . . . *either* of you . . . '

He didn't complete the sentence. He just gave us a mean look and walked out, grabbing his coat on the way.

Mother sat down with a weary shrug, and tears were trickling from her eyes. I went over to her and put an arm about her worn shoulders and soothed her.

'I can't help it, Rebecca,' she cried. 'I was hoping you'd lend me a few dollars to get the children some shoes. But now . . . that swine!'

'Don't worry about it, mother. I *can* lend you a few dollars. Actually I had ten dollars left . . . here's the other five.'

The look in her eyes was sufficient reward for giving my last five dollars to her!

★ ★ ★

I reported for duty long before the time given on the Monday, and, for my pains, I had to wait outside almost an hour until Michael Patterson arrived. He greeted me pleasantly and expressed his approval of my new dress and hair do, and then we went into the studio. He made some tea on a small stove first, then said:

'I think we'll get to work now, Miss Kay . . . or do you mind if I use your first name since we're to be working together quite a lot?'

'Not at all,' I told him.

'Great. I hate formality. And in return you use mine. Mike will do. Now, are we ready?'

He was so businesslike that I found it quite easy to dispose of my clothing without embarrassment. He said:

'First of all we ought to take a few studies for *Other World Magazine*. Let's think something up now . . . '

He didn't think for long. After a few minutes he went to a small door at the side of the studio, opened it, and from a cupboard there dragged a coffin.

He placed it in a suitable position,

smoothed down the white satin with which it was lined. He said: 'Only a papier-mâché one, but it comes in very useful to me. I'm afraid I'll have to ask you to lie in it, Miss Kay. Mind?'

'I — don't think so. No. Like this?'

'Fine. Just fold your hands across your chest and close your eyes . . . let me get the camera angle . . . yes, yes, that's it. Light — drapes — ready — hold it . . . '

'You can open your eyes and get out now, Miss Kay.'

I said: 'I thought we were going to use each other's first names?'

'Of course — I'm sorry. I forget these little things when I hit an idea . . . and this is a pip. *Other World* will lap it up.'

'What will you call it?' I asked curiously.

He grinned: 'There's only one name to fit it . . . a perfect name . . . *Dracula's Wife*!'

I murmured: 'Thanks for the compliment.'

'Sorry. But that's just the title for it . . . '

I said: 'What makes you do such

morbid subjects? Why not do something cheerful?'

'Rebecca, for eight years I did cheerful stuff. Girls beside rippling brooks, reclining on dark rocks, swimming in the sea — and I sold about ten percent of all my work. The reason for that was that about two thousand other competent photographers were doing exactly the same stuff. The competition was too great. Then one day I decided to try something — different. And here I am in a swell studio, with a secretary, and plenty of goulash. So now you know why I pick morbid subjects.'

'I understand now. Are you taking any more immediately?'

'Just one — but you'd better slip into your dressing-gown. It'll take a deal of setting.'

He worked rapidly, and I admired his inventive genius. He took two long papier-mâché rolls from his store-room and fixed them at the ends of a wooden framework. Then he strapped a handle to one of them, ran a thin aluminum plate beneath them, and adjusted his lighting.

'Right, Rebecca. That should pass for a

rack in the shadows, and that's good enough. Lie on the plate whilst I rope your wrists and ankles.'

I did as he told me, lay full length on the thin plate. He tied my wrists and ankles to the four ends of the roller with white ropes, stretched them taut, said: 'Yell out when this gets to be uncomfortable, will you?'

'It's that now.'

'Okay. Now try and simulate the expression of a woman screaming with intolerable agony — you get it?'

I got it; I screwed up my face and opened my mouth in a wide and silent shriek of torture.

He took the exposure and gave a sigh of satisfaction.

'Fine. I'll call it *Inquisition*, or something like that. You can get up now, Rebecca.'

'I wish I could,' I murmured. 'But I don't happen to be Houdini, or his daughter.'

'Oh, the ropes! Sorry — I forgot.' He released me and I got up and eased my cramped limbs. He said: 'You can get dressed again. I only need you for head and shoulder shots now. No hurry.'

I went behind the screen and started to dress. Whilst I was still climbing into my undies I heard the studio door open and a woman's voice said: 'Mike, *darling*! I thought I'd slide along and see if you were bankrupt yet. My, how *old* you look. You've aged three years in the last five days since I left you. But never mind, darling — admit you lose the bet, and I'll come back as your model . . . isn't that *perfectly* sweet of me, darling?'

'Is it?' I heard Mike grunt. 'Hmm. I don't admit I lose the bet, Marcia . . . not by any means! I said I'd take a working girl and make a first-rate model of her . . . '

'But, Mike, you just know it can't be done, you naughty boy. Come on now and admit it . . . I saw your advert in the papers — and obviously you haven't *any* model . . . '

'But I have,' said Mike, not without triumph. 'A very charming model, and far more photogenic than yourself, Marcia. In fact, I took a sample study of her when

I first interviewed her, and I have since sold it to *The Gentleman's Weekly* for a top fee. Are you ready, Miss Kay — Rebecca . . . ?'

'Hmm, Rebecca is it?' said Marcia, and there was a trace of bitterness in her voice. 'Fast worker in more than *one* way, aren't you, Mike darling? Who is Rebecca — *what* is she?'

I stepped from back of the screen and said: 'All ready, Mike.'

Marcia Storm was tall and languid, with a sophisticated hair-do and well-plucked brows. I remembered her from various pics in mags I'd picked up here and there. And at the first glance I knew she was going to be an enemy . . . scorn was written all over her well-made-up face!

4

Why Girls Leave Home

The first words Marcia Storm spoke to me betrayed something of her feelings — and I found the betrayal rather surprising. Mike didn't notice it, of course, but women do notice these things, and it was plain by the Storm woman's tone of voice. She said: '*Really!* Surely this — *this* isn't the young lady you're going to make a perfect model Mike dear, is it?'

'It is,' Mike admitted a trifle grimly. 'Why?'

'*Well* — ' she looked at me, said: 'My dear, you mustn't let Mike make a fool of you — he's so irresponsible. You really aren't the type for a model, are you?'

'I should have said exactly the same of you, Miss Storm,' I retorted. 'And yet you seem to have been extremely *lucky* with your career!'

'I suppose I asked for that,' Marcia yawned. 'Oh, well, if Mike wants to try, why not? I'm sure he'll realize he's only losing time and prestige eventually.'

Mike said: 'Here, here, if you two women are going to be round here you'll have to be a little more civil to each other. Marcia, you can say what you like, but I'm convinced I'm on the right lines. People will appreciate the youth and freshness Rebecca's going to bring to the game — they're a little tired of plucked eyebrows and finger-nails like talons — nothing personal intended, you know. But Rebecca's not a professional model, and that's why I think she'll bring something individual to the racket. See?'

'*Very* individual,' yawned Marcia. 'Oh, well, I *must* run along, dear thing. I'm going along to a party at Blossom's place in Greenwich Village . . . I expect you're too busy to come?'

'Is that where you were when we were supposed to have that date two nights ago?' enquired Mike grumpily.

'But of course it was. You surely don't mind me going to Blossom's, do you?'

'Knowing Blossom, and more particularly knowing her parties, I do,' grunted Mike. 'I'd rather you didn't attend unless I'm with you — her parties are little short of — well, orgies!'

Marcia patted his cheek with a lazy, gloved hand: 'My dear, how entirely *quaint* you are, aren't you? Wake up, darling. You know we girls have to get around to get our bread and butter . . . '

'Bread and butter's one thing — fur coats and diamond rings are another. If you see what I mean, Marcia.'

'Only too well, Mike boy. And there's something you ought to understand — if *I* don't object to your engaging another model . . . you mustn't try to tell me what to do and what not to do. Bye-bye, old dear, I'll give you a ring tomorrow. Goodbye, Miss — er — whatever your name is.'

I didn't acknowledge the remark. I turned away.

Mike followed her to the outer office, and when he came back he was frowning. He seemed upset about something, but didn't mention it to me. He said:

50

'We'll carry on now, Miss — that is, Rebecca. I'm sorry you and Marcia didn't get along, but I might have known she'd act like that. I'd love to know what the dickens makes me so fond of that confounded woman,' he added, half to himself.

We continued with the studies. He Kodachromed me in three different dresses, and then did a cover shot for *Glamour Mag*. At five o'clock he said: 'Well, that seems to be the lot.'

I went home thoughtfully, with instructions to report at ten the next morning.

As the next few days passed Mike seemed to draw more and more into his shell. Marcia didn't come round again, and from odd remarks Mike let slip I guessed she was causing him annoyance by her actions. And then, one night, he said: 'Rebecca, I wonder if you'd care to do me a favor?'

'Certainly, Mike. If I can.'

He frowned, took a step up and down the studio, said: 'I'd like you to go out with me tonight if you will. If you can call back here about six, I'll have finished developing, and we can go and have dinner somewhere. Later on we'll slip along to the Village — Greenwich Village, you know — and drop in on a party there.'

I faced him, said: 'I hope you aren't planning to make me a sort of retaliatory effort, for Marcia's benefit?'

He said: 'Why, no — well — forget it, Rebecca. I didn't have any right to ask you to do it.'

I smiled: 'It's all right, Mike. I'll come along with you. It may do Marcia some good. She certainly needs a lesson of some sort, and this is the only one which is likely to have any effect upon her.'

'Thanks, Rebecca,' he said. 'You're right about her needing a lesson — the fact is she doesn't really care for me at all. I may as well face the truth — I'm the one who's nuts about her! I don't care how, but I have to have her. You can see that?'

'I think so. I expect I'll be the same way about someone someday.'

'I expect you will. But about this party at Blossom's dump. Blossom is Blossom

Pennant — she's an artist, or likes to think she is. She has plenty of money and gives big parties in her studio down in the Village. All sorts of people get there, and you must stick beside me until you know how to look after yourself. The party may be distasteful to you . . . if you find it is, just speak the word and I'll take you home.'

'Don't worry about me,' I smiled. 'I'll get along all right.'

I went right home and dressed in the best things I had. Mike had told me the party was informal, and, in fact, that I was likely to see some very queer rigouts there. I wasn't ashamed to go along in my blue dress, with the little flower behind my ear, and the powder-blue shoes on.

I met Mike in town, and we dined quietly at a Chinese place he favored. I had never had Chow Mein before, and I didn't like it when I got it, but I didn't say anything.

At about eight we started out for the Village, and dismounted on the outskirts to walk leisurely along to Blossom's studio.

The streets were garishly lighted here and there by saloon and café signs. We passed a great many people with flowing ties and dreamy expressions. Some of them nodded to Mike, who seemed to be quite well known in the district. Mike said at length:

'Just around the next corner, Rebecca. Nervous?'

'A little.'

'Don't be. You'll be all right.'

He broke off as a tall, gaunt man in a flowing opera cape and dark Homburg hat came sweeping round the corner. This specimen suddenly spotted us, waved a bony hand towards Mike, swept off his Homburg to me, revealing a crop of flowing white hair, and a gaunt, high-cheeked face, and then hurried towards us.

Mike murmured: 'Here's one of our characters now. He used to be an actor — played Hamlet along Broadway, and he's never forgotten it yet. He's a decent old stick for all that. Try to humor him.'

The character came striding up as if making a dramatic entrance. He bowed deeply and profoundly and said, in a deep voice: 'Ha! Prithee, I trust thou art well, Michael?'

'I'm living, Orvel,' agreed Mike. 'And you?'

Orvel pulled a long face, and sighed wearily: 'They have forgot me, Michael. Aye, the wretched ingrates have forgot me. No longer do they recall the cheering masses which once worshipped at my feet. No longer do producers seek me out for their choicest plums — alas, my fame is like an empty drum — my cup of bitterness is overflowing. Bring on the hemlock, executioner . . . I may no longer tarry . . . '

Mike cut in hastily, stopping his exclamations and violent gestures: 'This is my model, Miss Kay . . . Rebecca, this is Orvel Barrat, the *great* actor . . . '

Orvel Barrat subjected me to a close scrutiny, then swept off his headgear again. 'Charmed. A pretty wench, Michael. I trust thou art well, Mistress Kay?'

'I'm very glad to meet you,' I told him. 'I've heard a great deal about your wonderful performances . . . '

'Thank you, my child. Ah, alas, those days can be no more. If I were to tell you the part a responsible producer offered me for a forthcoming production, you would shudder that true art could be so maligned . . . '

'What was the part?' questioned Mike.

Orvel Barrat glared all round, then lowered his voice: 'The hind legs of a comic horse!'

'*No!*' we echoed.

'Othello . . . Hamlet . . . Shylock . . . Henry the Fifth . . . ah, me! But I told him — I told him most *firmly*. 'Sir,' I said, 'Know you not to *whom* you are speaking? Is it for *this* — this ignominy, this desecration of my aestheticism, is it not tragic? I, who was stormed by cheering multitudes. Magnificent in my role of this downright insolence, that my agents bid me offer my services to you?' He said: 'The job pays forty bucks a week, and your legs are long enough.''

'I guess you told him about that, too, eh?'

'I most certainly *did*. 'Sir,' I said with dignity, 'if you offer me *that* position once more, I will do something *drastic*.''

'And did he?'

'He did. And I *did* something drastic, Michael.'

'You did? What?'

'*I took it*. We open Thursday at the Globe Theatre in, of all things, burlesque!'

We laughed, and walked on together. Orvel was going along to Blossom Pennant's party, too; not, as he told us, because he liked the damned things, but because he had to eat, and there was always food at Blossom's. Looking at the color of his nose, I judged it was not so much the food . . .

Blossom Pennant's studio was a magnificent affair on the fifth and top floor of the building. It consisted of five rooms, one of which was a bedroom, one a sitting room, one a kitchen, and two studios. It was in the studios that the party was held.

I don't think, ever in my entire life, I have seen such a motley collection of people. They were Bohemian, most of them, dressed in everything from negligees and furs to painters' smocks and evening dress. They were mainly from the Village itself, but there were a few from uptown, like Mike and myself. There were authors, artists, poets, architects, musicians, heaven knows whats, and even a scruffily attired curbside artist.

Many of them had gained fame with their work; others hadn't even got their feet on the bottom rung of the ladder. In addition to these, there were many models, male and female, some whose beauty was purely superficial, and others who were truly beautiful in their own style, stately or gay.

Marcia was chatting in one corner, sitting on the knee of a fat poet in a morning suit with a wilted carnation. As Mike and I entered she rose and walked over: 'Why, Miss Kay, isn't it? And Mike — how delightful to see you here. I had no idea Blossom *knew* Miss Kay.'

'She doesn't. But she asked me to bring along a friend,' Mike said shortly. 'Who's the guy?'

'Him? Oh, just some punk poet, darling. He's been telling me some of his sonnets . . . as far as I can see he seems to have lifted them bodily from Shakespeare. But he's rather *jolly* company, and his knee is so much more comfortable than dear Blossom's chairs. Really. Well, I must push along . . . mind you don't *lose* anything here, won't you, Miss Kay?' she said, smiling sweetly.

I went red, but kept my temper. I said: 'In view of *your* example, Miss Storm, I'll be most careful.'

She simply smiled and drifted back to her poet. But under the smile it was plain she was raving mad that Mike had turned up in a gathering of her friends with another woman.

I was introduced to a tall, fair man, with a serious and well-formed face and a muscular figure. He seemed a pleasant enough person and he was obviously enthusiastic about me.

'Mike,' he said, 'I must paint her sometime . . . now, don't keep her all to yourself, man. Don't be greedy.'

He then lost himself in the throng, and Mike murmured: 'That was one of the more successful artists. His work sells well. He does nude studies in oils . . . and he's very particular about his models. Only uses the best. You should feel flattered.'

'What's his name again?' I enquired.

'Reeves — Gilbert Reeves. A good enough chap except that he's too wrapped up in his self and his work. He's good, and he knows it, and he lets everyone else know it.'

A straight stick of a woman with cropped hair, a monocle and mannish tweeds marched over: 'Nice to see you again, Mike,' she said, in a deep voice. 'Nice, nice. Who's the lady, eh?'

Mike performed introductions. The woman turned out to be none other than Blossom Pennant. When she left us I said to Mike:

'I don't wish to seem rude, but who on earth gave her the name of Blossom? Pennant I can understand — but Blossom . . . never.'

He grinned: 'She is slightly faded, isn't she? A regular old prune. But I believe Blossom is her given name. Perhaps she changed for the worse later in life.'

I spent an interesting half-hour meeting

odd people. There was the author of *Passion Forever*, a book I hadn't read and didn't want to, and there was the creator of the Daffy Dahlia cartoon strips, an item I always enjoyed in the Funnies. Then there was a slim, grave-faced Englishman, who composed popular songs with an American flavor, and who, Mike told me, had a very bad crush on Marcia.

Mike seemed to be looking round for someone, without any luck. He said at length: 'I thought Mornia Garish would be here. I wanted you to see her — she's an example of the finest model in the business. She can command practically any salary she likes to name for a sitting . . . I've used her once, and Reeves has recently done an oil with her. The Pennant woman often pays her fabulous sums to pose for her, but of course Blossom's work never sells, and never will. If she had to do it for a living she'd starve to death. Sure to.'

'And isn't this Mornia Garish here?'

'Doesn't seem to be — funny, because I've never yet known her to miss a party at Blossom's.'

We forgot the perfect model then. The fun was waxing fast and furious . . . a little too furious for my liking, although I said nothing. Drinks were disappearing down various throats, and some of the men had discarded jackets. Marcia was up on a table, much the worse for whisky, performing a modern version of the Can Can to riotous applause and grabbing hands from the men. Others of the girls were sprawled out on the lounges round the room, half drunk and in a maudlin state, not caring much what they did or who was watching them. It was, as Mike had once remarked, an orgy.

The conversation became even more ribald; suggestive songs were trundled out and given an airing; more whisky and gin was poured. Over in one corner Orvel Barrat sat like a rock in cape and hat, eating sardine sandwiches and drinking claret. Nearer to us Marcia did a Hula dance now, and chanted a disgusting chorus. A half-clad girl came rushing from one of the other rooms, shrieking with laughter. A bald-headed old lecher followed her waving a silk stocking. They vanished in the kitchen, and there were screams of glee from behind the closed door.

Reeves, the artist, sat aloof from it all, regarding the goings on with an air of utter disgust. Mike and I sat together, he staring at Marcia's antics with fists clenched, and I trying not to look too shocked at the struggling figures which were draped revealingly across the lounges and on the floors. Mike snapped as Marcia threw her garter to one of the men: 'Damn her! This is her way of paying me back for bringing you.'

'Perhaps we should go ... ' I suggested. He didn't seem to hear me. He sat with knotted fists.

The revels went on, quickening, until I was forced to stare at the window blinds to prevent myself blushing with shame at the wretched depravities committed by members of my own sex. Some of the more decent people left when the orgy started; but all too many remained to keep the fun going fast and furious. Over it all presided Blossom, not indulging herself, but watching the others and wearing a little smile — a smile which seemed to me to be entirely false, as if she was laughing at the fools her friends could make of themselves, and feeling herself superior. A gross dark, mauling Italian grabbed out at me as he whirled past in the arms of another girl . . . his hand caught my leg and dragged me from the chair I was sitting on. He wouldn't let go. Mike went after him, punched him neatly in the jaw, and took me from him. No one worried and suddenly the door opened and a young man dashed in. His face was perspiring as though he had been running to bring some news . . . his eyes were wild with excitement and alarm.

He barged through to the center of the throng and shouted:

'Hold it . . . *listen* . . . '

'Sit down . . . '

'Give it a rest.'

'Go home, Harper.'

There was a chorus of yelling and two girls seized the young man and pulled him across the room. He was yelling:

'You idiots . . . listen . . . '

They dragged him down, rumpled his hair, parked him in a corner and gave him a drink, and then sat on his knee. Angrily he threw the girls aside, shouting: 'I didn't come here to act the goat tonight. I came for a reason . . . I came to *warn* you . . . '

Blossom heard his words, stood up, and went across to him. As he spoke rapidly to her her face became as alarmed as his own. She hammered on the piano and called in a strong voice: '*Silence!* Listen everybody . . . '

A hush fell over the room; at last the revelers realized something was seriously wrong. Marcia said petulantly: 'Well, what is it, Harper?'

'It's Mornia Garish,' he said, his words echoing loudly through the sudden silence. 'She's been found — *murdered!*'

5

Killer at Large!

In an instant, from being a noisy, rowdy arena, the Greenwich Village studio was converted to a place of absolute silence. There could not have been less noise if everyone had been suddenly struck dumb!

The young man called Harper — a nice-looking young boy with a red, round face — stood panting and staring round after he had dropped his bombshell. But the first to break the silence was Marcia. She said, in a stunned kind of way: 'My God! *Another!*'

Blossom Pennant said, quietly: 'How was it done, Harper?'

'Strangulation — like the rest. There'd been a struggle.'

Reeves was no longer sitting quietly where he had been. He was on his feet, his face almost grey. He muttered: 'This is the *fifth* — the fifth in two years!'

'And all of them top-line models,' joined in Harper. 'It must be the work of a maniac. Always models — seemingly he catches them alone — and strangles them . . . '

Reeves said: 'What makes you think it's a man, Harper?'

'It must be. Didn't the police say that they believed a woman would be incapable of exerting such tremendous strength?'

Blossom put in: 'Have the police arrived? Are they there?'

'Not yet . . . I found the body. I was here, you remember. I started wondering where Mornia was, knowing she'd intended to come along later in the evening. When the fun started I slipped out and walked the two blocks to her place. I knocked, but didn't get any answer. Then I found the door was unlocked and I went in. Mornia was lying by a small coffee table on the floor — her dress was ripped and the place was all disordered. The blue marks on her neck told me the rest . . . '

Mike now joined the conversation. He said: 'You said you came here to . . . *warn us?* Why was that?'

Harper glanced round. He said: 'Because there's going to be a great deal of trouble . . . about this murder. Someone from *this party* killed her!'

There was a stunned silence. It was Blossom who recovered first.

'Isn't that a silly thing to say? What makes you so certain someone here did it?'

Harper fumbled in his pocket and produced a crumpled cigarette end, which he threw on top of the piano. He said: 'That . . .'

Reeves exploded: 'Good Heavens! Was that at the scene of the crime, Harper?'

Harper nodded: 'And everybody here knows that Blossom imports this type of smoke for her guests at these parties. There are open boxes of them all over the studio . . . look! The way I see it, the killer lit a cigarette, then sneaked out smoking it. He went the few blocks to Mornia's place and, being someone she knew, she naturally invited him in. Perhaps they talked a moment or so, then he took her by surprise, attacked her, and killed her. In his rush to get out he forgot the cigarette end on the ashtray . . . '

'Then you are saying the murderer is in this room *now*?' said Orvel Barrat.

Mike grunted: 'That's stupid. A lot of people left before the rowdiness started. It could have been anyone of those. Or the killer may not have returned after the job was done.'

Reeves added: 'Another thing — that cigarette may have been taken at a previous party — it may even be one Mornia herself took.'

Harper said: 'Think so? Then take a look at the tip — you all know how much lipstick Mornia uses — that is, used. Any smoke she had would be certain to be well marked with red. I noticed her lips were heavily made up, too. There isn't a trace of make up on that butt. So it isn't likely to have been Mornia's, is it?'

Blossom said: 'What makes you so anxious to warn us all? Why didn't you telephone the police and hand them this clue?'

Harper flushed. 'I didn't like Mornia Garish and I'm not making any secret of it,' he said. 'She was too high and mighty.

I almost went on my knees to get her to pose for a study — but she wouldn't. I couldn't offer her enough. I thought if I went and got to her tonight I might be able to persuade her to change her mind. But if someone's killed her I think they may have good reason, and mainly because I can count everyone in this room a casual friend. I thought it as well to warn you . . . '

Reeves said suddenly: 'Harper, this mustn't get out — about this cigarette end. You hear? Some of us here have reputations to think of — if the details of this — party — came out, we'd be ruined! What do the rest of you think?'

Blossom Pennant said: 'Frankly, I think we should call the police at once, without any delay. This is serious business; if the person who is killing all these models can be apprehended we ought to do every-thing in our power to help the police. It may be any one of us next — you, or you, or even myself. What's to stop the killer turning to others besides models?'

Harper growled: 'I say the same. I believe someone in this room — or someone who has been here — committed the murder. And I vote we send for the Homicide Squad right now.'

Reeves looked upset, but he drew back, confessing himself overruled. Orvel Barrat murmured: 'Harper, my dear young friend, as you are so insistent someone here murdered the poor young lady, how about *yourself*? You are the only one who has been to her place as far we know.'

Harper growled: 'Don't be a fool . . . '

Barrat said: 'Doubtless you will be able to persuade the police that they too are fools, when they tax you with the same question.'

Mike said: 'Wait a minute — who can prove definitely that they haven't left this room since the party started?'

Reeves said quickly: 'I've been sitting here all the time. Everybody could see me . . . '

'I saw you,' said Orvel Barrat. 'But not *all* the time. Don't you remember I passed you coming up the stairs about forty-five minutes ago, just as I was going out?'

Reeves seemed flummoxed. 'Er — yes,

that's so. It was very stuffy. I went to have a breath of air . . . '

'So you say,' put in Harper. Reeves scowled darkly. Harper went on: 'And why were *you* going out, Barrat? I remember seeing you standing outside the door when I went out to get Mornia. What was *your* reason?'

Barrat said: 'Simple, my dear fellow. I, too, found it somewhat unsettling up here — I had had a little too much to drink and felt — queasy. I thought a little air would help me to overcome the sickness.'

Blossom Pennant observed: 'Air seems to have been to great demand tonight, doesn't it? In very great demand. Perhaps that was why Marcia vanished for about fifteen minutes right after she'd done that Can Can for the boys. Eh, Marcia?'

Marcia looked startled. She said: 'I — I went to powder my nose . . . '

'Funny. Couldn't you have powdered it equally well here?'

'Very well,' snapped Marcia. 'If you must know, I went along to the bathroom on the outside landing. I — I snapped one of my shoulder straps of my slip and had to take off my dress to tie it again. Naturally I didn't want to do it here . . . '

Blossom said: 'Really? Why not, pray? Judging by your dance, you didn't seem to mind *what* you did here.'

'If you're accusing me, how about yourself?' grated Marcia with a mean look on her face. 'You were missing from the room for some time yourself!'

'I was in the kitchen cutting more sandwiches,' said Blossom calmly.

'Can anyone prove that?' sneered Marcia.

'No. Roddy Truman was there whilst I did it, but he was fast asleep with that Martin girl. I didn't disturb them . . . but for that matter *either of them* might have sneaked away and done it without us knowing. We were far too excited to know who was here and who wasn't. The fact is that anyone in this room might have gone out, killed Mornia, and got back without being missed.'

Barrat murmured: 'That is so . . . '

'No,' I protested; 'I was here all the time . . . so was . . . ' I had been going to say Mike, but — here Marcia cut in:

73

'Mike wasn't. He left the room.'

'That's right,' agreed Mike. 'I did. But that doesn't say I killed her, does it?'

We gazed round at each other in hopelessness. Harper said: 'I think I'll call the police. I'd better. Mike ... ' he glanced at Mike: 'Why did *you* leave, the room?'

'For the reason you intend to leave it in a moment,' Mike said calmly. 'I went to phone someone.'

'Can whoever you phoned prove that?'

'No!'

'Why not?'

'If you insist on third degreeing me, because they happen to be dead ... '

'You went to phone someone who was — *dead*?'

Mike smiled grimly: 'Yes. I went to phone Mornia Garish. I particularly wanted Rebecca to meet her. I didn't get any reply, so I gave it up as a bad job and came back again. Does that satisfy you all, or do you imagine I killed her?'

'It may satisfy us,' said Reeves. 'But will it satisfy the police? I still say let's hold on and say nothing ... '

Blossom shook her head. 'No. It's far too dangerous a thing to do . . . all those five girls who've been killed off in the past two years have been noted as the finest models in the Village, and who knows when the killer may strike again? He seems to have a yen to murder the beauties . . . '

She broke off and stared at Harper; he was staring at Reeves. His mouth was open, foolishly. He said: 'That reminds me of something — something I hadn't thought of before . . . Reeves, every one of those girls had one thing in common . . . '

Reeves licked his lips, said: 'I don't see . . . '

'Don't you? Then I'll open your eyes . . . *every one of those girls had been painted by you just prior to their deaths!* And you started working here about two years ago, didn't you? And isn't it rather funny that every girl you have so far portrayed has met a nasty death only a month or so later . . . ?'

Reeves had gone white. He croaked: 'It's ridiculous. Why should I — what purpose would I have . . . '

'I'm not a mind reader,' snapped Harper. 'But maybe you have a fixation . . . you know, that whoever you paint mustn't be done by anyone else . . . '

Blossom cut in: 'That's fool's talk. Harper. It may be sheer coincidence that Gil happens to have painted the identical girls who've been killed. And I'd advise you not to be foolish enough to point out the fact to the police, or Gil may care to do something very drastic about it all.'

Harper walked out to find a phone without saying anything more. But his accusation had caused more than one person in that room to look askance at Reeves, and with a muttered: 'If the police want to see me they know where to find me,' he took his hat and coat and walked out. The rest of us waited.

★ ★ ★

By the time the police had finished their preliminary investigation it was turned half-past one in the morning. They got precisely nowhere; for it seemed that the clue of the special brand of cigarette was useless in one way, since any of the people at Blossom's party could have dropped it, and even Mornia herself could have had it on hand.

Surprising facts came out, however: Orvel Barrat had a motive for murdering the girl — not a strong one, but nevertheless a motive, especially to an egomaniac like he was. It seemed that this Mornia Garish had been continually taunting him, every time they met, with being a ham actor. Orvel had often said he'd like to murder her, being sure the world would be a sweeter and cleaner place for her absence.

But an even stronger motive was possessed by a Swedish radio script writer, who had had an illicit affair with her and had been thrown over flat. He didn't deny his love had turned at once to a deep hate.

Harper had the motive of his spurned offer to her to sit for him. It was suggested that possibly he'd done the killing on the spur of the moment.

The fact that Reeves seemed upset and

worried and had gone home abruptly seemed to interest the police.

And it was dragged out that Marcia positively loathed Mornia, for she considered without Mornia being around, she, Marcia, would get the plums of the fees and offers. And certainly, next to Mornia, she was considered the top of her profession.

Blossom Pennant didn't deny that Mornia had been over-popular as far as she was concerned. She couldn't have put a name to it, but she said it was just generally the high-toned actions and way the Mornia Garish woman had had of going about things.

In addition to these, my biggest surprise was when Mike admitted to having a motive for murdering Mornia!

He didn't make any bones about it; said he'd cheerfully have strangled her if he'd thought she was at all worth it. It seems that Mike had once had a friend, deeply in love with Mornia. In her usual slap-happy way Mornia had had intimacies with this friend, and had then thrown him over. His pleas had been of no avail, and being a more sensitive man than the Swede, he had taken his own life, leaving a suicide note for Mike explaining things.

In fact, I was about the only person who hadn't known Mornia Garish in that party, and even I wasn't free of suspicion. The police suggested I might easily have left by the back stairs whilst Mike had been going to the phone.

But the really *awkward* point that cropped up was that whilst eight or nine people had had motive and opportunity to murder Mornia, not one of them had motive for murdering the other five models who'd been killed, obviously, by the same man — or woman.

So the inspector, at length, told us we could go home, but that none of us should leave town until he gave the okay. He said we might be wanted for further questioning, and asked us to hold ourselves in readiness. Then he went over to see Gilbert Reeves with a determined look on his face, and the party split up, none of the guests feeling in the mood for any more talking right then.

Mike took me home in a cab, and on

the way he was thoughtful and distracted mentally. Once he turned to me and said: 'Of course, you don't think I did it, kid, do you?'

'Of course I don't, Mike. I'd sooner believe I'd done it.'

'Thanks. You're a good kid. I noticed Marcia looked at me once or twice as if she suspected me . . . but I'm through with her. She went *too* far tonight — I realize now that I'll have to do without her — have to *make* myself . . . and I've been thinking, Rebecca . . . that if . . . if you don't mind, you could help me . . . '

I said: 'I don't mind, Mike. Glad you've seen the light.'

He dropped me in front of the tenement. I went up the stairs thoughtfully . . . and bumped into father standing on the top step, *belt in hand* . . .

6

Another Reason Why Girls Leave Home!

Oh, yes, I knew what was coming to me right then. It wasn't just the fact that I'd come home late — I knew that by the magazine he was holding towards me, open at a page which contained a glossy art study. For the art study happened to be the first one of me that Mike had taken — me, supposedly hanging from a rafter, and it was titled: Nadir.

I halted on the third step from the top and stared up in fright. He'd been drinking, and when he'd been drinking — which was almost always — he was a vicious degenerate. The belt was held firmly in his hand, buckle end free. His fingers were tight clenched about the magazine, crumpling the paper in their fierceness. He snarled: 'Get inside!'

I darted past him, rushed into the room, through into my bedroom, and slammed the door and locked it. I heard him walk in and hammer on the door. He shouted: 'Open this door!'

'No, father. I'm tired — I — I'll talk to you in the morning.'

He stopped hammering. I heaved a sigh of relief, heard his footsteps retreating across towards mother's room. I hastily slid off my coat, hat, and new dress, and got into bed wearing my slip.

And then I heard him fumbling at the door, and I remembered with a shock of horror that the key to his bedroom fitted the lock of my door. I sat up desperately — the door flew open, and he walked in, putting on the light. He stood looking at me as I sat huddled in the bedclothes with terrified eyes. He swished the belt in the air once or twice.

He grated: 'It's a good job the kids sleep with your ma and me. We won't disturb them with our little chat . . . ' and he shut and locked the door behind him.

He came right over and said: 'Get out of bed, you little bitch, you cheap little gutter slut. Get out of it . . . '

I got out of it; I stood trembling in my

slip. He eyed me, then threw the glossy mag down on the bed. 'Well? Is that what you call developing? Or when you said you were going to work at developing, did you mean your body?'

I colored. Remained silent. He snarled: 'D'you think it's nice to have that sort of thing shown me by the boys down at the pool hall? The boys who buy that kind of dirt — showing me my own daughter without a stitch on? You shameless bitch!'

I tried a last resort: 'The — money's good. I — I get thirty dollars a week.'

'So old Weinbaum told me tonight,' he grunted. 'I owe you something for telling me you only got ten. I suppose you and your blasted mother meant to have a fine time with the extra twenty you'd have cheated me out of.'

'Why should you have it?' I said, growing angry in spite of my fears. 'What did you ever do to earn a cent for the last fifteen years? It's always been poor mother who's worked in this house.'

He didn't flare up; his face stayed wrathful, but he spoke in a low tone — a dangerous tone. I knew it too well: 'So you feel like getting uppity, do you? Well, I might have let you keep the job as it pays good money — but not now! I've been waiting up for you three hours . . . you know my orders are for you to be in by ten. It's nearly two . . . just where have you been until now?'

I said: 'I couldn't help myself — I went to a party in Greenwich Village . . . '

'With who?'

'My — my new employer,' I faltered.

'Did you? And he kept you until now, did he? Why, you dirty little tramp, is this what I've tried to bring you up decent for? You good for nothing . . . '

I cried: 'There was nothing wrong . . . I swear there was nothing wrong. It was just that something happened which . . . '

'I daresay something did happen, but I'll teach you not to start that game — you hear? I'll show you what'll happen to you if you come to play those games with me.'

And before I could scream an explanation he sent the belt whistling through the air and full across my stomach. I gave a shriek of agony and fell backwards across the bed, trying to cover my face with my arms. He rained blows on me, the heavy buckle cutting through the thin slip, biting into my flesh . . .

I screamed, and the more I screamed the madder he got. I fell off the bed a tangle of arms and legs, and he followed me round, lashing savagely at my back; his temper was gone . . . his eyes were small and red and insane. He followed me up, battering at my defenseless body, every nerve of which was shrieking as loud as I was myself with the torture . . .

Dimly I heard a hammering on the door and mother's voice shouting in panic; father ignored it, went on thrashing me; and suddenly the blows ceased and I was lifted gently to the bed and my torn underthings covered with a sheet.

Mr. Weinbaum and Billy, and mother, and the two kids were all in the room. Mr. Weinbaum had firm hold of father, and the blood-smeared belt was on the floor.

Father had lost his insane rage, but was still glaring at me wildly.

Old Weinbaum said, above my sobs:

'Come on out, Harry, you fool. You shouldn't ought to go thrashing the poor girl like that. You might've done her some injury. Come on out, let her be. You've lost control of yourself, man.'

He started to lead father out; but father turned at the door and glared back at me. He snarled: 'That's a foretaste! If you come home late again you'll get more . . . much more. I won't damn well stand for it, see? You hear? I won't have any daughter of mine carrying on with them artist fellers. And you can give your job up at that rotten bastard's place tomorrow.'

Then the door closed behind them.

Mother got a bowl of water and chased the two kids and Billy out of the room. Then she took off my tattered under-things and bathed the bruises and wounds gently. There were tears in her eyes, big tears, and I joined her.

'Rebecca, you must leave here,' she said between sniffs. 'You can't spend your life any more subject to the demands of that beast. God, however did I happen to marry a man like that?'

I patted her arm as she bathed me. 'I'll leave, mother. I'm determined that he won't get me to drop this job. I'll go first thing in the morning. I don't have to report until ten, and by that time I can find a little place and take my stuff over. I haven't much luggage, thank Heaven.'

'And I won't tell him where you've gone . . . perhaps when he sobers up he'll have enough sense to leave you alone. The bad, wicked beast!'

'Don't worry any more, dear. And I'll send you ten dollars a week to help get things for the kids. Don't let him know about it. Keep it to yourself.'

She smiled through the tears, said: 'I don't know where you were tonight, Becky, but . . . you *were* all right, weren't you?'

'Yes, mother. I give you my word.'

'That's enough for me. Do take care of yourself. I can trust you — I always have. Don't you come here anymore. I'll come and see you sometimes, and bring the children over. But don't get in his way again — he isn't responsible for what he does when he gets in this condition.'

She finished bathing my hurts and said: 'There, is that better?'

'Lots. They feel soothed now. Good night, mom . . . ' She kissed me and went out. I locked the door and jammed a chair under it. I lay awake, aching all over my body. I wondered how on earth I'd come to have so much trouble so suddenly. Losing Billy's friendship, turning everyone against me, tangled in a murder case, and now turned out — voluntarily of course — of my home. Not that I'd miss the dirty tenement. But I would miss mother and the two children. It was a long, long time before my eyes closed . . .

When I came down at half-past eight the next morning, father was still in bed, sleeping off his drunken bout. Mother had a nice breakfast ready for me, and there were signs that she had been crying during the night: redness about the eyes and cheeks.

I ate silently, and rose at last to go. She had my things all packed, and she pressed twenty dollars into my hands: 'I'd been saving it — for an emergency.'

'I couldn't take it mother . . .'

'Don't be silly, Becky. *This* is an emergency. You'll need it. Later on you can pay me back, dear . . . now hurry before your father gets down. I'll tell him I don't know where you are if he asks.'

I kissed her and held it for a long time. She gulped, then whispered: 'I'll say goodbye to the children for you when they get in from school. Goodbye, Becky . . . let me know how you get on, dear.'

There was a lump in my throat as I walked away from the dirty tenement. It's surprising how even a wretched, vermin-ridden hole can seem a wonderful place, just because someone dear to you lives there. Then, too, I was really afraid for mother — afraid that father would suspect she'd helped me to pack and run, and would take it out of her. How horrible life can suddenly become. Once I had thought I would be on top of the world when I'd got out of the sweatshop . . . but now . . . I'd never had such a case of the blues. I felt sure life wasn't worth living.

I stopped at the library. I glanced down the rooms to let section of the paper. I was looking for something in Greenwich Village, where rooms were usually cheap, and where I'd be in more constant touch with new opportunities for advancing myself as a model. At last I plumped for an address which advertised a two-roomed apartment to let over an artist's studio.

I took the trolley down there.

The place was neat and clean, and the woman who opened the door to me was large and motherly-looking. She wobbled with the weight of her fat as she climbed the rickety stairs to the top rooms, and panted a great deal as she unlocked the door and let me in.

'Here you are, my dear: Not very big, but reasonable. You can do your washing and cooking in my kitchen — be a bit of company for me, I expect.'

They were tiny rooms, and not over-furnished. But they were neat and clean, and far superior to the dirty little place I'd had at home. I said: 'They're lovely. How much are they?'

She peered at me keenly. Said: 'You're only young, aren't you? From out of town?'

'I — no. Well . . . '

She hazarded a shrewd guess. 'Left home, maybe?'

I nodded. 'My father — I couldn't get along with him.'

She said: 'Hmm. That fresh bruise on your face — has that anything to do with it?'

'I . . . '

'You needn't answer if you don't want to. I'm not being nosey, dear, but I'm not supposed to let rooms to girls under age. But I think I'll make an exception in your case . . . you look done in. The rooms are ten dollars a month, my child. Can you manage that? If not . . . '

'Oh, yes,' I said eagerly. 'I'll let you have a month in advance now.'

'Not a month . . . stay a few days first and see how you like being away from home. Maybe you'll want to go back . . . people get awful homesick. I know. I ran away when I was a girl.'

'I don't think so. But I'll do as you say. Thank you.'

She patted my shoulder: 'Cheer up. Things are never as black as some of the bum artists round here paint them, you know. And if you ever feel the need of company, my kitchen's on the bottom floor, and my name's Elsie. Elsie Tate. I'll be glad to see you any time.'

'Thank you, Mrs. Tate.'

'You'd best call me Elsie, dear. Makes me feel younger. There's only one other boarder here — he has the studio on the ground floor. His name's Reeves . . . '

'Reeves?' I said in surprise. 'Gilbert Reeves?'

'You know him?'

'Casually . . . through a friend of mine. The photographer I work for.'

'Mr. Reeves is a queer man — a bit conceited, between you and me and the ears in the walls. But I've always found him pleasant enough, for the little I see of him . . . well, dearie, I'll leave you now. Any time you feel like a cup of coffee, call on me.'

Mike was at the studio when I got downtown. He nodded to me, seemed a lot more cheerful than the previous night. He said: 'No more news about the murder yet, Rebecca. Marcia rang me up last night to say she was sorry for making a show of herself . . . said she couldn't help it, the drink went to her head.'

'Oh. Did you . . . ?'

He chuckled: 'I did. I had the pleasure of hanging up on her, without bothering to listen to her explanations. I expect she's furious about it now.'

The studio was arranged for the shots he intended to take. A canvas roll had been lowered at one end of the room, painted like a rough stone wall. Just before the camera were a half-dozen dummy rifles propped up facing the wall on a high trestle, with only the muzzles in range of the lens. The blinds were drawn and one small arc was lighting the set, making a mixture of light and shade.

He said: 'Okay, Rebecca, this is the only undraped study. When you're ready stand against the canvas, tie this black cloth over your eyes, and spread your arms out. Facial expression blank. The idea is to get the muzzles of the rifles in the picture, with their business ends pointing towards you. I'll call it 'At Dawn,' or something like that.'

I undressed behind the screen, and spent a couple of minutes examining the bruises and cuts on my body. I hoped he wouldn't notice them too obviously. Perhaps the lighting would not be strong enough to reveal them plainly. But he noticed them at once. He stared at me for a minute, whilst I felt embarrassed, then said: 'What's wrong, Rebecca?'

'Wrong? Oh, you mean the — the marks . . . nothing, Mike. I — I just fell out of bed . . . '

'Did you? On your back and front at the same time? Or did you fall out twice?'

'I — I'd rather not talk about it — *please* Mike. If the marks will spoil the shot perhaps we can leave it? They aren't very noticeable.'

'Not much,' he grunted, puzzled. 'But they won't spoil the shot kid. Maybe they'll enhance it . . . I'll call it 'Mata Hari,' and bung it off to *International Spy* magazine. But how on earth did . . . '

'Mike — please.'

'Okay, okay, I'll mind my own business. Ready?'

He took the shot and I got dressed

again. When I was through he showed me a letter from one of the women's magazines.

'I sent them a sample of one of those cover pics I took of you. Seems they'd like me to do a series modeling the latest designs in women's wear. They want you to pose for all of them. They like the freshness of your appearance . . . so in view of that I think I'll be able to raise your ante to forty dollars a week. I guess you could use some of that money at home?'

'I — I'm not staying at home any longer, Mike. I left this morning. Now I've got a place down in the Village over Reeves's studio.'

He raised his brows, but didn't question my reasons for leaving home. He just said: 'With Mrs. Tate? Old Elsie? She's a good sort. She'll make you comfortable there. And if you're on your own now the forty will be handier than ever.'

'Thank you, Mike.'

'How about going out to lunch? It's too late to start any more work at the moment, and I'm feeling peckish. Okay? Remember, you've a responsibility to me now. You agreed to help me forget Marcia . . . '

I got my coat and hat on and we left the studio. We were just leaving the outer office, when father walked in, scowling!

7

Mike Gets Tough

Mike didn't know who father was, of course. He stopped courteously, and if he felt surprise at seeing such a scruffy person in his offices, he didn't show it. Personally I was momentarily struck dumb through my fear.

Mike said: 'Good morning. Anything I can do for you?'

'No,' father grated. 'I'll do all that's to be done myself. I came for *that* cheap slut . . . my daughter. I told her she wasn't to come back here, see, but she did. I thought the hiding I gave her last night had taught her I won't be played with, but it seems like it hasn't. Her mother said she'd left home, and didn't know where she was, so I came round here where she works, hoping I'd find her.'

During all this Mike's face had gone hard. He shot a glance at me, then faced father again. He said: 'Are you referring to Miss Kay?'

'Who the hell d'you think I'm referring to? Greta Garbo?'

Mike nodded slowly and carefully: 'I see. So you thrashed her last night, did you?'

'Wouldn't you have? When a girl her age gets to stopping out until two in the morning she isn't up to any good, I tell you. She was with some no-good feller, I expect.'

'She was with me,' said Mike coldly.

Father thrust his jaw forward pugnaciously: 'Oh, was she? Then I'm glad I gave her what she asked for. I don't like the look of you, nor the way you talk . . . an' in future keep your hands off my girl, you hear . . . ?'

Mike colored a little. Father snapped: 'Come on, you,' to me. I hesitated. He said: 'D'you hear? I said come on — I'm taking you back home and locking you in until you come to your senses.'

I shook my head, determined to make a stand for it. I said: 'I'm not coming with you, father. Don't make any trouble

98

about it. I've left home for good.'

'For whose good?' he snarled, the brute showing itself in his face, the gorilla in him rising up. 'Not for your own, I say. But you can stop being so hoity toity an' outraged and come along with me — or do I have to make you?'

I whispered: 'You daren't . . . '

It goaded him into action. He took a quick step forward, caught my wrist in a grip that made me cry out, and slapped me hard across the face. 'Now . . . ' he grunted, and got no further. For Mike had gone white, taken a quick pace himself, and shot his clenched fist to father's jaw. Father gave a yelp and went down.

Mike stood over him, breathing hard, and I stood cringing against the desk, behind which the secretary was all of a dither.

'Get up,' rapped Mike grimly. 'Get up, Mr. Kay. I wondered how Rebecca'd come by those bruises and cuts — now I can see it all plainly. Any man who can do that to his own daughter is long overdue for a first-class thrashing. I'll make it my pleasure to give it to you . . . get up!'

Father lay where he was, rubbing his unshaven chin dazedly. A furtive, fearful look had stolen into his eyes, and for the first time in my life I realized contemptuously that in spite of his brutal dealings with mother and myself he was a rank coward! It's generally the way, but I'd always thought father could hold his own — now I saw him in his true colors.

He was afraid — almost shaking with fear — of Mike.

That single powerful blow had taken away all his braggadocio. He was a weak, cringing fool, unable to raise a hand against a man who might be his match.

After all I'd been through I felt sorry for him. I said: 'Mike, don't hit him again. Just make him go . . . '

Father spat out: 'Abduction, that's what it is. I'll have you in court for this. There's a law which works on fellers like you — procuring young women . . . you bastard!'

Mike had cooled off. Now he murmured: 'I'll be satisfied to go to court about this — you may have forgotten there's also a law which prevents a man ill-treating his children. I happen to have a plain camera shot which shows the bumps and bruises on your daughter's body. And when I go to court that study goes with me!'

Father's malevolence suddenly faded. He'd forgotten that. He knew the way he'd thrashed me was good enough to get him three months or a heavy fine . . . and he hadn't the money to pay a fine!

He seemed uncertain for a minute, and he almost sniveled in his anxiety. Mike said: 'Look here, I don't want to take this any further, and I'm pretty sure Rebecca doesn't either. Give me your word you'll leave the girl alone in future, and I'll forget about raking the matter up. But break your promise any time, and I'll have you in front of a judge before you know what's hit you! What do you say to that?'

Father was completely beaten. He mumbled: 'You win. The girl can have her own way. But from now on I don't recognize her as no daughter of mine, do you see? That's all I got to say.'

'Doubtless she'll be well pleased with

that arrangement,' Mike smiled. 'And now you'd better go . . . '

Looking exactly like a whipped cur, father sneaked away.

* * *

We went again to the Chinese Restaurant Mike liked. Down there many models gathered, together with photographers, artists and newspaper men. For all that it was quiet and dignified, nothing like the more riotous haunts of the Village itself. We ate American food this time, and I found it really well cooked.

We had hardly finished our coffee when a tall figure lounged across and sat down at our table. It was Marcia!

'Mike, darling,' she breathed. 'So nice to see you again. You're quite a stranger, aren't you?'

Mike looked uncomfortable. 'What do you want, Marcia? Anything in particular?'

Marcia looked pained: 'Well, my dear . . . I've decided that our little quarrel should be patched up, you know. We've both been foolish, but in future we can try to please each other a little more . . . admit it, Mike, darling — you miss me.'

'I do,' agreed Mike, and I felt a little shiver of annoyance at Marcia's triumphant smile in my direction. 'I miss you a great deal, Marcia. I haven't to worry about you these days. In fact, I can honestly say I haven't been so *happy* since the day I first met up with you!'

Her mouth was wide open in her astonishment.

'*Mike* . . . '

'Sorry, Marcia, but that hold you had is broken. Well and truly broken. Thanks to your own display at Blossom's, and thanks to Rebecca here, I've realized my mistake. That isn't very flattering, but I see no reason to mince matters. I'm through, Marcia, for *good*. I mean it.' Her face was a mask of rage and hate. He said, cynically: 'If you betray your feelings so openly, Marcia, you'll have people laughing at you.'

She hissed: 'I'll make that little guttersnipe sorry for her part in this

— and I'll make you sorry too, Mike . . . If you think I'm the type you can throw over you're wrong. I could kill you both for this, you . . . '

She hissed out a stream of bad language, and Mike raised his eyebrows, said: 'Marcia! Really! Is this the way a prominent model deals with a broken affair? I didn't think you knew such words!'

She gave him a final glare of hate, and turned away.

Mike looked at me closely when she'd gone. I said: 'Mike, you shouldn't have thrown me up at her . . . that's the thing she most disliked . . . '

'Why not?' he said quietly. 'I'll be frank with you, Rebecca. The reason I'm able to do without Marcia is because I've fallen in love with you. I had, I think, from the time you walked into my studio looking for a job — perhaps before that — perhaps when I read your letter I knew.'

I kept my eyes down. I didn't know what to say. He went on:

'You aren't under any obligations to

me, and you don't need to return my feelings. But you may as well know how I do feel, so that there needn't be any misunderstandings between us. I didn't want to tell Marcia as much as I did, but I couldn't help it. She asked for it — and besides, if I hadn't she'd have kept pestering me. She wouldn't have realized I really meant what I'd said — she couldn't believe that a man who'd been in love with her could transfer his affections to any other woman like that.'

I was listening to him, but at the same time my mind was busy. I was wondering how *I* really felt towards *him*. I hadn't yet loved anyone — Billy had been a friend and nothing more — and I found it hard to analyze my feelings with regard to Mike. Did I love him?

Was that why I'd been so anxious to help him throw off Marcia, was that why Marcia had never been civil to me, because she knew at once what I didn't . . . was that why I had felt that little pang of annoyance when he told me Marcia had phoned him after the party, and why I had felt the same way when he had said, at first, that he missed her?

I looked at him through my lashes. He was toying with his cup, not looking at me. I looked at the clean, strong sweep of his jaw, the cool grey eyes, the even white teeth, and the tiny lines round his eyes. I tried to get to the bottom of what I really did feel for him. Couldn't be sure whether it was gratitude for having lifted me out of my rut and protected me against father, or whether it went deeper than that . . .

Apparently he didn't expect me to profess love for him, for he grinned at me and stood up: 'Time we got along. Got a cover page to do for *Amateur Photographer*. Finished?'

I nodded, and we left the restaurant.

* * *

'I'll slip round later, when I've finished developing,' said Mike. 'I know the address.'

'I'd like that,' I told him. 'Not too late, Mike. It's past nine now.'

We'd had rather a long day. A rush

contract had come in for some illustrations for a technical mag., and we'd stayed late to get them finished. I'd been hopping in and out of different fabrics the entire evening, and I felt very tired. But I wanted Mike to come round later — I knew I was going to feel strange and lonely in my little apartment the first night, and Mike would be able to cheer me up until bedtime.

He carried on developing, and I left.

I decided to walk; the night was cool and exhilarating, and I thought a stroll would revive my tired nerves. I took it easy, gazing round at the city, and the brightly dressed 'dames and guys' who thronged the sidewalks, going to theaters, dances, jive parlors, bowling alleys, and a million other places. Cars flew past with the more fortunate citizens in evening dress, heading for the uptown niteries and opera houses and concert halls, and other places which probably the hoi polloi wouldn't have patronized if they'd had the chance.

I had a queer feeling that I was being followed after a time. I couldn't have said why, but it persisted. I glanced round very sharply once or twice, without seeing anything unusual about the gay throng behind me and all round me. I shrugged and passed on.

But when I reached the Village later the feeling was still there, but even stronger now. I was being followed.

It was miserably dark in this section, and as I passed the various eating places and tiny shops and tenements, I glimpsed a dim figure behind me. I heard his steps on the sidewalk, stealthy steps, slowing when I slowed, quickening when I moved faster.

Fearful thoughts assailed me: I remembered the murdered models and shuddered. Could I have been picked out as a likely victim? Was it possible that the killer had chosen me as a suitable subject for his next excursion into murder?

Shivering, I started to hurry; once I passed a patrolman, who gave my legs an appreciative glance, and I thought of stopping and requesting his assistance. But no — I may have been just imagining things, and I'd have looked a fool if my fears had been unfounded. Besides, I was almost at my apartments, and within a few minutes I would be upstairs and behind locked doors.

I reached the studio, noticing as I did so that the lower floor, which Reeves occupied, was in darkness. From the kitchen at the end of the long passage came the sound of Mrs. Tate, the landlady, singing in a loud but unmusical voice. I toyed with the idea of paying her a visit, then laughed it off and hurried upstairs.

I gained my rooms and rushed inside; listened with the door half-open.

Steps were coming slowly, jerkily, drunkenly, up the stairs!

Panting, I closed the door softly, fumbled for the key to turn it. It was missing!

On the outside, perhaps!

I listened again. There was silence.

I opened the door cautiously and looked out.

Father was standing on the dimly-lighted landing, swaying like a tree in a hurricane. His face was red, he was terribly drunk, and he was peering about through his bleary, close-set eyes!

I took a chance and reached for the key — and it wasn't there, either! At the same instant he saw me, and lurched towards the door. I whipped inside, slammed it shut. I braced myself, but it was hopeless. One heave of his shoulders and the door flew open, and father lurched in.

'*Now!*' he wheezed, approaching me as I backed away around the table. 'Now! So you thought I was afraid of your young man, did you? Thought you were going to get it all your own way, eh? But you aren't . . . oh, no! I've been waiting two hours outside that studio place for you coming out . . . and I've followed you here to have a little chat. A little chat with *this* . . . '

He was unbuckling his belt with sickening certainty. His face was a drunken leer. I stammered: 'Leave me alone. Get out. You don't know what you're doing — Mike will . . . '

'Mike,' he spat. 'I suppose that's the swine who you was with in that studio, eh? I'll take care of Mike. I'm getting a bunch of my friends to help me take care of Mike. Mike won't be out of hospital for a long time when we've dealt with him. And after I've attended to you I'll give your mother something for helping you . . . anyone'd think you didn't have a good home, coming running away here.'

I picked up a chair, held it aloft. I said: 'If you dare . . . '

He made a sudden jump; I threw the chair. It missed him by an inch, smashed against the door. His mouth started working, and he blurted: 'You little swine . . . I'll . . . '

I ducked back into the bedroom. I screamed. He came after me, leering, stroking the belt. The look in his eyes was terrible. I drew up gasping against the wall . . . he snarled: 'Now!'

And from the doorway of the other room Mrs. Tate's voice said:

'Dearie me! Is that you, Rebecca?'

'Oh, Mrs. Tate, help . . . ' I shouted wildly. 'It's father . . . he's drunk and . . . and he'll do some damage. Get some help, please . . . '

The next second she appeared in the bedroom doorway, took in the scene, and moved quickly towards father.

'Get out of here,' she said belligerently. 'Get out until you sober up. I don't wonder the girl left home if you're her father!'

Father ignored her, just thrust out a hand and pushed her aside. His eyes were still fixed on me. Mrs. Tate recovered from the push, and as he raised his belt she threw herself on him, caught the end of the belt, and hung on. He turned on her with a snarl, trying to wrench it from her grip . . . she yelled: 'Get away, Rebecca. Get away, child, before he gets loose. I can't hold him for long. Get a patrolman . . . hurry!'

Father suddenly let go of the belt and came for me with his bare hands. Mrs. Tate went over backwards with a yell. I took my courage in both hands and made a frantic rush for the door.

I got out, almost tumbling down the stairs. He came after me, not twenty-feet behind. At the bottom of the stairs I overturned a small hall stand and, as I rushed through the front door, had the satisfaction of hearing his curse as he tripped over it. I panted over the road,

112

reached the sidewalk. Only one pedestrian was about. He was fifty yards from me . . . father came tearing through the door into the street, spotted me, and blundered across blindly. The heavy truck loaded with beer came round the corner without any warning. I saw the driver's white face. Saw father's sudden look of terrified realization.

And then there was a sickening scream and the truck passed on.

8

Reeves' New Model

The truck didn't even stop. The driver was most likely scared out of his wits that witnesses would be able to state he'd taken the corner at a fantastic speed, and without sounding his horn.

It rolled off in the darkness in a burst of speed, and when I saw what was left of father, I just fainted there and then.

I came round again to find myself in my apartment; Mike had arrived, and was holding me in his right arm; a fat-faced patrolman was watching from one corner. Mrs. Tate was bustling about with a bottle of smelling salts she'd been using on me.

Mike said: 'Okay, Rebecca, take it easy . . . I'm sorry this happened . . . '

The patrolman said: 'Mind answering one or two questions, Miss?'

I passed a hand across my head.

'If you don't feel up to it just now, I'll wait . . . '

'No, it's all right. Please ask them.'

He consulted his notebook, said: 'We want to know if you got the number of the truck?'

I shook my head. He went on: 'This lady here tells me it was your — father. Is that so, Miss?'

'Yes. Yes, it was father . . . '

I wondered if Mrs. Tate had told anything more. The patrolman said: 'Mrs. Tate tells me you'd just left the house when your father called to see you. She told him you'd gone, and he hurried out after you. Then he was unfortunate enough to run into the truck, according to a pedestrian who was about a hundred yards away from you. He says he didn't see too clearly, but that's how it looked to him from what he could see. The truck drove on. Is that right?'

I nodded. He said: 'Can you give me your father's address and name?'

'Harry Kay, floor five, Potter Tenement Building, Brooklyn.'

'Thanks. We'll have to inform your

relations . . . mother still alive?'

'Yes. Officer — would you mind very much if — if I told her? The — the shock — '

'Not at all, Miss. We may need you later, so be ready for a call. That's all for the moment. Good night.'

He left the room, and I looked at Mrs. Tate gratefully. I said: 'Thank you for covering up the facts . . . '

'That's all right, honey. I didn't think you'd want the truth known, and it wouldn't have done your father any good to have told it. Your young man came up just after the accident. Do you feel better now, dearie? Like a cup of coffee?'

We had a cup of coffee. I felt a lot better then. Mrs. Tate handed me father's belt, which he had left when he hurried out, and I put it in a drawer.

Then I turned to Mike: 'Mike, would you mind calling a cab, and taking me over to my home?'

'You intend to tell your mother — tonight?'

'I think so. Yes, I'd rather get it over with. Father was just as beastly to her as he was to me, but when you've lived with a man for twenty-five years I suppose anything like this comes as a terrible shock . . . but in the long run she'll be better off. I know it isn't right to speak evil of the — the dead, but I can't think of one solitary good thing father ever did as long as I've been able to think for myself.'

Mike patted my arm and went out to call a cab.

We rushed over town. It was turned eleven, and I was feeling sick and tired. The memory of seeing father lying there with his — but I can't describe that. It was too horrible.

Mother was still up when we reached the tenement, but the kids were in bed. An anxious look spread over her face as I came in, and she said: 'Rebecca, you shouldn't be here. Your father was raving wild this morning. I haven't seen him since . . . he went out to look for you.'

'I know, mother. He found me . . . mother . . . '

The lines of worry deepened in her worn face. She said: 'He didn't harm you *again*, did he? By God, if he did I swear

I'll kill him . . . I'll . . . '

'No, he didn't harm me, mother. I . . . sit down.'

She noticed Mike in the doorway behind me, and turned a questioning look on me. I said: 'This is my new boss, mother. Mike, my mother.'

I could see there was something warm in Mike's eyes as he gripped the thin hand she held out to him. She said: 'I'm glad you have someone to look after you, Rebecca. Sit down, Mr. Patterson. I'll make some coffee right away.'

I said: 'Forget the coffee, mother. Listen, I have a shock — well, a surprise for you. I — I don't know how you'll take it. But you'll be — well, better off, in my opinion.'

She clutched anxiously at my hands. 'Rebecca — what is it?'

I blurted: 'Father . . . '

'Your father? You've seen him? Is he in trouble?'

'Worse,' I mumbled haltingly. 'He's had an — an *accident*!'

She was stiff and still; her hands fell away from mine.

She said: '*Accident*? How — how bad?'

I said, in a low voice: '*Very* bad. A truck — he didn't see it — he's *dead!*'

She stared at me for almost a minute. Then her voice came in a whisper as she clasped her hands together: 'Dead?'

'Yes, mother . . . '

She said: '*Thank God!*'

The words came right from her heart, and knowing what a gentle woman she had always been I could see just what a life father had led her to make her greet the news of his death like that in front of a stranger. Apart from the usual brutality, he always was a peculiar man in every way, and often, when I had been just a child, I had heard her screaming out once or twice in the night.

'Dead,' she repeated fervently. 'For ten long years, ever since he began to ill treat you and your sisters, I've prayed with all my heart for him to be taken. And he has . . . God is *good*. Everything will be different now. I'll be able to give the babies what they need, and I won't have to hand over my wage packet to him every week . . . how did it happen?'

There was not a trace of pity on her

face as I told her. She just listened intently, nodding every now and then. At last she said: 'He came to thrash you again . . . and the devil claimed his own! Will you be coming back home again, Rebecca?'

'No, mother, you're overcrowded even with three. Let the two kids have my old room and you make yourself comfortable in the big room. I'll stop down in Greenwich Village — I've a nice little place, and the landlady's a dear. She helped me to dodge father. If she hadn't, heaven knows what would have happened to me.'

'He was mad,' mother said quietly. 'He was mad, Rebecca. He should have been shot — like a mad dog. He couldn't take his drink and hold it. It was that way ever since the day I married him. He wanted a slave, and I've been that — if only I'd known what he was sooner — if only I hadn't ever married him. I've *lost* all that part of my life . . .'

I told her: 'Don't worry, mother. From now on you can have it easier. You needn't work so hard . . . I'll send you twenty dollars a week . . . '

'No, Becky child, I couldn't . . . '

There was a lot of argument. But in the end I persuaded her not to protest any more. She wanted me to stay at home for the night, so I took Mike to the door at last and stood in the entrance to the hall with him. There was a dim light burning, and even as we looked at each other it was turned off, and we were in darkness.

I said: 'Mike — '

'Yes, Rebecca?'

'I've been thinking over what you said today . . . about me.'

He laughed lamely: 'Oh, forget it. You don't have to give me an answer if you'd rather not. I can always wait. Maybe in time . . . well, maybe in time I'll grow on you, like a wart . . . '

I said: 'Mike — you have grown on me. I knew tonight, when I regained consciousness, that I'd never felt as safe anywhere as in your arms. What I want to tell you, Mike, is that — I love you too. I know that now . . . but I don't expect I'd have had the nerve to tell you if that light hadn't gone out like it did.'

He was breathing faster; moved nearer to me. 'You really mean that, Rebecca? It isn't that you're feeling lonely and depressed . . . ?'

'No, it isn't. I *do* love you, Mike. Very much.'

Then his lips were against mine, and I knew what real love was for the first time in my life. For a long time he held me close. Then he laughed shakily and released me: 'Good night, Rebecca . . . '

'Good night, Mike. And thanks for all you've done for me.'

'Thanks for all you've done to *me*,' he said softly, and then he was gone.

*　*　*

When I reported for work the following morning, Mike gave me the day off to get settled into my new apartment. I went round town buying little odds and ends I would need, and it was almost three in the afternoon before I got back. Going along the hall I bumped into none other than Gilbert Reeves.

'Miss Kay,' he hailed me pleasantly.

'This is a pleasure. I understand you live here now?'

'That's right, Mr. Reeves. Just above you. I've been here a couple of days.'

'I'm sure you'll be very comfortable. Mrs. Tate is a kindly soul. I've been here for two years, and I've never had any reason to be dissatisfied. My studio is just here, you know. Perhaps you'd care to look round it sometime? I may say I'd like the privilege of having you sit for me, soon, if you can manage it.'

'I'd love to see some of your work, Mr. Reeves,' I told him. 'I understand it's awfully good.'

He wasn't modest: 'Frightfully. Of course my real work is yet to come, but even the rough work I've turned out is far, far better than anything anyone else round here is capable of.'

I said: 'So Mike always tells me . . . have you been to Blossom's lately?'

He said: 'Not so far. She hasn't decided when she'll give another party yet. I fancy she wants to let the affair of Mornia Garish cool down. That was a *funny* affair.'

123

'Very funny. Well, I must rush, Mr. Reeves . . . '

He said: 'Wait a minute. How about coming down today? No time like the present, is there? I'm doing a study at the moment that may interest you . . . and while you're here I'll show you the portrait of Mornia Garish I did. What do you say?'

What could I say? I said: 'In about an hour?'

'Fine, fine. Don't bother to knock. I'm frequently absorbed when I'm working. Just walk in — I'll leave the door for you.'

'Won't your model mind?'

He laughed. 'Why should she? You're a model yourself, aren't you? And a woman? No, it'll be all right. Help yourself.'

I left him and went upstairs. I walked into my room and for a moment I thought I had either walked into the wrong rooms or was dreaming. For they had changed — marvelously.

Instead of the neat but well-worn furnishings, there was a brand-new walnut suite in the sitting-room. A thick carpet lay on the floor, into which my feet sank deeply, and chintz curtains brightened the windows.

I walked dazedly into the bedroom: here again the transformation was astounding. The somewhat drab bed had gone, and in its place was a cozy single with polished headboard. The windows were brightened up by colorful curtains, and the rug at the side of the bed was warm and luxurious. The dressing-table was new and matched the bed itself, as did the wardrobe and the tallboy.

I had to pinch myself to make sure it was real.

Then I noticed the note on the bed, went over and picked it up. It was addressed to me. I opened it, took out a sheet of paper. It read:

Dear Rebecca, — Don't get mad about all this. I didn't like you to be living in squalor — you deserve better. That's why I arranged to have this done whilst you were shopping. Take it as my first gift — let's call it an engagement present. It'll come in handy for our own place later on, I expect — all except the bedroom, dear.

MIKE.

So it was Mike's doing. I'd wondered why he'd acted so strangely and secretively that morning, and had insisted on me having the day off to do some shopping. He'd been supervising the transformation scene in my rooms, doubtless with the aid and conspiracy of Mrs. Tate.

I didn't know how to thank him — didn't know quite if it was right for me to accept such wonderful presents from him. But then I looked at the note again, and read the bit about being engaged over and over, and felt happier than I had for a long time. Yes, I'd marry Mike. I knew surely there wasn't, and wouldn't be, anyone else for me.

I bounced on the bed, and sat on the divan and played round like a school kid with a new toy.

Then I remembered that I'd promised Reeves I'd slip down and see his studio below, and I decided I didn't want to disappoint him because he'd been so nice about it.

And for no reason, a sudden feeling of nervousness descended on me. I couldn't say why I felt like that, except that Reeves had been a number one suspect at Blossom's party. Quite a lot of his friends thought he may have had a hand in the murders . . . and the idea of walking into his parlor like a fly gave me a nasty sensation.

I laughed it off; after all, there was nothing definite against Reeves, and even if he *were* the man responsible for killing five other girls, it didn't say he'd take a chance of killing me in broad daylight in his own studio.

I went downstairs, remembering what he'd said about being absorbed in his work, and just walking in. To tell the truth, I was a little curious as to who his new model would be — it seemed to me that after five of his past models had already perished it would need someone with considerable nerve to pose for Reeves. Or someone who imagined they were quite capable of taking care of themselves.

I opened the door and went in. I was in an outer room, with very little furnishing. Here, covered by dust sheets, hung oils of nudes, still life, pastoral scenes, and stormy seas.

I went round them, raising the dust sheets and examining them. His work was good — that was evident even to me, who didn't know an oil from a water, hardly — it had something individual, which stood out, whatever he tackled. He seemed to favor dark, bold sweeps with a strength of line which should have belonged to an altogether burlier and brawnier man.

I toured the canvases, inspecting each. His subjects were every bit as queer as Mike's photographic studies were. Amongst the titled canvases were some weird, grotesque effects.

'Harlem Wolf' one was called, and it depicted a dark-faced wolf, dressed astonishingly in a zoot suit, padding silently after a short-skirted young lady.

Next to it was another: 'Grandfather's Chair,' this was terrifying in its realism. He had depicted a white-haired old man screaming in a paroxysm of terror as guards strapped him to the electric chair. The way the eyes started out of the old man's skull gave me the shivers.

Next were some surrealistic studies he had evidently been trying his hand at. One was of an angular mass of grey lines of different shades converging in the right-hand corner, over a pale golden background, with a section of skyscraper jutting into the left ear of a man who resembled an emaciated monkey. He had called this 'Subway' . . . and apparently, as an afterthought, and for some unknown reason, had added a pair of misshapen girl's legs.

But his more serious work, the landscapes, the portraits, the nudes, also had something unusual about them. The expression, the peculiar way he had woven his colors together, his sense of balance and perspective. All were different from anything I had seen before. As Mike had said, Reeves was certainly a great artist.

I walked towards the inner studio, pushed open a swinging door, and went in.

Reeves was standing sideways to the large rear window, making a rough of the portrait he was engaged on, which was a nude. The model reclined on a piece of draped velvet, facing the window her back to me. But as I entered she turned for an instant . . . and murmured:

'Miss Kay, isn't it? Come to pick up a few tips on modeling, no doubt?' And having said that, Marcia turned her head away again.

9

Change of Heart

So Marcia Storm was Reeves's newest model! Of course, Mike had told me Marcia was pretty well up in that game, but I hadn't quite expected Reeves to fancy her somehow. Maybe it was just cattiness on my part, but to my eyes she looked far too modern and hard for any real artists to want to paint.

Reeves glanced up from his work, and his face lit up when he saw me. He said: 'Ah, Miss Kay . . . '

'I hope I'm not disturbing you?'

'Not in the least. As a matter of fact, I had already decided to finish for the day. The light isn't very good.'

Marcia said: 'Is that all then, Gil?'

'Yes, that's all, Marcia. Same time tomorrow.'

He didn't ask her to stay — in fact, his tone of voice suggested that he'd prefer

131

her to leave as soon as possible. She shot me a glance and vanished behind the screen.

He pottered round showing me some half-finished work until she had gone; then he smiled, said: 'I'm glad you could come, my dear. I've been rather struck ever since I saw you at Blossom's place.'

'Struck?' I queried hesitantly, knowing what a forthright lot these artists were.

'Oh, I see. No, by struck I mean struck on your possibilities as a subject for my brush. Since Mike seems to have got in first I'm afraid I'll have to be contented with simply painting you. How do you stand with regard to freelance posing?'

I said: 'I can't say . . . I'm supposed to be working full time for Mike . . . '

'Have you a contract?'

'No, nothing like that. Just a verbal agreement.'

'Then you are perfectly free to pose for whoever you like.'

I shook my head: 'I wouldn't care to offend Mike,' I told him. 'He's been very good to me . . . '

He chuckled: 'It gets a little deeper

than *that*, I think, doesn't it?'

I blushed: 'Well — we're engaged.'

He nodded. 'Marcia will be furious about that,' he grinned. 'She hasn't been able to talk about anything other than the way Mike seems to have lost his senses running round with you these last few days. You must watch Marcia — you haven't any idea how spiteful she can be.'

I smiled: 'Thanks, but I think I can take care of myself as far as Marcia's concerned.'

He showed me over to a covered canvas in the corner. He switched on a roll light over the easel and said: 'This is the canvas I really wanted you to see . . . the one of Mornia Garish . . . you know . . . '

He pulled aside the dust cover and stood back, watching me intently. The portrait took away my breath for a moment; the slender, wild-eyed woman, arms thrown back, hair awry, body nude, and with a look that was half insane laughter, half intolerable misery, on her startling features.

He said: 'I call it 'The Face Beneath'.'

'I — I don't know *what* to say,' I stammered.

'You don't? What are your reactions to it?'

I said: 'I'll be frank, Mr. Reeves. I think it's *horrible!*'

Strangely, he looked quite pleased at those words. He said:

'It is meant to be, Miss Kay. The exposed soul of a loose woman. The yearning, the pity, the terror, the insanity, the wild laughter, the grey misery of her life.'

'I can see that . . . the work itself is wonderful. You've managed somehow to convey all that. But it's — I don't know: well, frightening. Frightening in its truth.'

He threw the dust sheet over again. Said: 'Mornia was the ideal model for it. Her life was no text book on morals. I'm glad I completed it before she — died.'

He turned and took me over to the one of Marcia on which he was working. This depicted Marcia, face a mask of terror, eyes protruding from her head. She was lying upon a divan, and from the head two sinewy, dark hands crept from shadow and were fixed viciously on her throat.

Reeves said: 'That is even more horrifying?'

I shivered: 'The subject . . . '

'I know, it's in bad taste so soon after Mornia's death, isn't it? Very bad taste. And yet — the truth is I can't help it, I have to go on doing it. It isn't myself. I'd stop the whole thing here and now if I could. It's that impulse, that uncontrollable driving force in me which commands that I should do a portrait of this nature. I think the matter's been weighing too heavily on my mind.'

I turned away from the gruesome, sketchy outlines. I felt I shouldn't care to see the completed work.

Reeves murmured: 'That, of course, has convinced you *I'm* the murderer? Or if not convinced, at least driven a fresh nail into the scaffold of suspicion. Hasn't it?'

I said: 'It was bound to do that, wasn't it?'

'Naturally. Marcia is a little afraid I think. I think she eyes me askance now and then. But she is so eager to go ahead in her career, and, without being unduly boastful, I may say that sitting for me will help her considerably.'

'Then she *isn't* afraid?'

'Of me . . . ?'

'Oh, no. Of posing for you? After what has happened to your previous models?'

He shrugged: 'Perhaps she is afraid. It is as I said. She considers the risk justified by the reward. She has made no objection to being portrayed like this.'

I was silent, examining the oils he was showing me one by one. Many of them seemed to have been done by a younger, more immature hand. These were scenes of wonderful beauty, lakes and chalets, misty lanes and rolling oceans, painted on small canvases. I said: 'Somehow these don't seem like your present work.'

'No,' he agreed. 'They aren't. They were done, most of them, more than eight years ago. When I was a rolling stone, gathering very little moss. I had just enough of an income to roam, paint what I liked when I liked and where I liked. Somehow I hate to dispose of these

— they remind me of the days when I was free to come and go, the days before I lost the little I had, and when I was not forced to paint for a living. Italy, Venice, Austria, Switzerland, Spain, Portugal, Sicily, Greece, India, Africa . . . I could go on forever. But two years ago the best part of the shares I held went smash, and I was forced to think of settling down and earning money by my brush. So — here I am, in Greenwich Village.'

Curious now, I asked: 'But after painting the beautiful side of things as you have, what made you turn to the grotesque and frightening?'

'Quite simple,' he smiled. 'Like your friend Mike. I found the demand for that type of thing far exceeded the supply. Added to which I have always had a strange, unaccountable impulse to seek the weird and the bizarre.'

His reference to Mike caused a thought to cross my mind which jolted me. Mike, too, was fond of subjects which had a morbid trend. And if Reeves's choice of studies suggested to me that he might be the killer, why not Mike's? I thrust the idea away and felt almost ashamed of my disloyalty.

Reeves pattered on; about the advantages and disadvantages of the artist's life, about the compelling desire to splash the world on to canvas, which gripped and refused to be denied. And the eternal striving to produce something which would stun and amaze the world, which would gain acclaim and reap rich reward for its painter. He had some derogatory remarks to make about the Mona Lisa — in fact, since I had been a model I had heard many of these struggling artists criticize that masterpiece most unkindly. Whether it was jealousy, or whether they genuinely believed the work overrated, I could not say. He went on to deride Turner in a mild sort of way, and to point out the merit of his own skies, and their superiority over any ancient or contemporary work. He most certainly was an egomaniac.

And I wondered once or twice, when I looked into the strangeness of his glowing eyes, if that was the *only* kind of maniac he was!

At last he glanced through the skylight,

which formed the roof of the large bay windows, and said: 'Beginning to get very dark. Ah, well, it's been most enjoyable having you, Miss Kay. I must paint you — the moment I've finished Miss Storm. If I ask Mike if he minds you posing for me, will that be quite agreeable to you?'

'I think so . . . but you'll have to guarantee I don't go the way of your other models, Mr. Reeves,' I smiled.

He didn't seem to take it in the light spirit it was intended. His face darkened and he bit his lip pensively.

'Miss Kay, I can't understand what's happening to the girls I use as my models,' he said, shaking his head. 'It's beyond me why they have all been chosen by someone to meet terrible fates. If I thought there was any danger of more of my models being strangled . . . I honestly believe I'd take to landscapes or surrealistic work. But surely it can't go on forever? There *is* a law; there are police; they *must* do *something* . . . they must! Or are we to understand that — Marcia — will be the *next* to go?'

★ ★ ★

I was thinking about Marcia as I went upstairs. Consequently it gave me a shock when I walked into my rooms to find her sprawled languidly in a chair.

She made no effort to greet me, or to get up. She sat there smoking, and insolently flicking ash onto the new carpets.

I confronted her calmly. 'Well?'

She drawled: 'I expect you want to know to what or whom you are indebted for this unexpected honor? Don't you, my pet?'

I said sharply: 'I do. I don't remember inviting you over for a social call.'

'You didn't. I came to give you some advice . . . '

'About what?'

'About *whom*,' she said. 'About Mike. Mike Patterson.'

I turned round, found a chair, and sat down. I said: 'Will it take long? Because if so, you'll be able to give it to me in front of Mike himself when he arrives.'

'No, it won't take long. Not long at all.' She stood up and crushed her cigarette in

140

the ash tray. She glanced about the apartment. She said: 'Don't you find it rather difficult to buy stuff like this on a *model's* money, dear? Or have you some way of *supplementing* your income — I shouldn't be surprised.'

I snapped: 'Say what you have to say and get going. I don't like you and you don't like me. I don't like you because you've tried to make a fool of Mike, and you don't like me because I *have* made a fool of *you*! So we have little in common . . . '

'We have one thing in common,' she sneered: 'Mike! You say you love him, and so do I. I may have tried him a bit too far, but I don't mean to lose him. I won't lose him! Certainly not to a dirty little guttersnipe like yourself.'

'Thanks,' I murmured, refusing to be drawn.

The fact that she couldn't irritate me seemed to drive the cool assurance from her, leaving her a sleek, dangerous woman. A woman scorned, who would stop at nothing to gain her ends. She surveyed me narrowly, then hissed: 'Listen to me. I'll make your life a hell unless you leave

141

Mike alone. I'll be even with you for coming between us. I loathe you — and when I loathe anyone I always find some way of doing them an injury.'

'Are you threatening me?'

'I'm warning you. Watch your step, little Orphan Annie. If you keep getting under my feet you'll get *trodden on*. Do you understand? *I'll* tread on you, my pet — with hobnailed boots! Get away from Mike, I tell you. Leave him to me. He may try to kid himself he's got me out of his hair, but I'll be back there again. It's only a passing phase with him, a period of feeling he can do without me and like it. He can't. You'll see about that. Within two more weeks he'll run back with his tail so far between his legs it'll touch his nose. And in spite of the way he's treated me lately, I'll take him back — gladly.'

'Why? You don't love him; you know you don't.'

She regarded me pityingly. 'Love, my pet, is a peculiar word. It can mean any one of a number of things. There are degrees of love. Different kinds of love. And my kind of love is not quite the same brand as yours.'

'Your brand isn't love at all. The only person you love is yourself, in the fullest sense of the word. Your love is physical. There isn't anything mental about it. You love for the thrill of being loved by the man of your choice. You know that as well as I do. But if the man of your choice wouldn't have you, you'd quite easily forget and turn to someone else. You're in love with men, Marcia — not any *one* man. But because you've been pushed out with Mike, you're determined to have him. You found he wasn't so firmly corralled as you'd hoped. And now you're making a belated attempt to get him back.

'But you're too late. You're shutting the stable door after the horse has been stolen. I don't mind telling you that any chance you did have with Mike went the night you made a show of yourself at Blossom's party. From there on he saw a little sense.

'You won't get him back, Marcia. I'm telling you . . . and I know I'm not just talking spitefully. You *can't* get him back!'

Her green eyes glittered: 'Can't I my pet? What makes you so sure?'

I shot my bolt: 'Because Mike and I are *engaged*. If you want to know where this furniture came from, I'll tell you. It was his engagement present to *me*. And I have an idea it won't be long before we're making it the basis of our home!'

She had gone white. She stammered: 'You liar!'

I threw her the note from Mike. She read it with flashing eyes, and when she had finished threw it down with temper on the floor. She almost snarled: 'Mike seems to forget he and I were engaged! There's such a thing as breach of promise suits! I'll sue him for every last shirt button he possesses.'

'You'll do nothing of the sort,' I told her contemptuously. 'You wouldn't have a leg to stand on. Mike can get ten or twelve witnesses who'll testify about how you've carried on. You'd be lucky to even get costs. And on top of that you'd most likely get a reprimand.'

For more than a minute she stood and stared at me, her face working with rage. Then, without another word, she turned and walked out.

I heaved a relieved sigh, adjusted my hair and make-up and wandered downstairs to Mrs. Tate's kitchen to have a chat until Mike arrived to pick me up and take me out.

Mrs. Tate was still as fat and red-faced as ever. I had never seen her in a bad temper — and never did. The day she failed to find something worth singing about had not dawned. She gave me a cup of coffee and we sat beside the electric fire drinking it. After a little casual talk she said: 'It isn't any of my business, dearie, and I daresay you'll set me down as a nosey old woman, but just what is the argument between yourself and that Marcia Storm creature?'

I smiled. 'Nothing of importance. It just happens that she's lost Mike to me, and she's living up to the old proverb about Hell having no fury . . . I'm not worried about it.'

She said: 'She did seem upset. I couldn't help overhearing when I bent by your keyhole to tie my shoelace, accidentally on purpose, if you see what I mean. I thought perhaps you were in trouble again.'

'I'd hardly call it trouble, Elsie,' I laughed.

'Just the same, I'd be careful if I were you. I don't know much about the Storm girl — but I don't need more than a look at her to know she'd stoop to anything. She's the type. I can tell, honey. I've lived a lot longer than you, and I've seen more of life — and if that happens to sound hackneyed remember that it's none the less true. I've seen women, hard calculating women, with features which are beautiful, but over them has grown that same tell-tale mask that I can see on Marcia Storm's face! It's something no amount of make-up can hide — beautiful eyes, but when you look deep they're like pools of frost. Red smiling lips, but if you've a mind you can detect the cruel little lines at the corners. Long shapely fingers — tipped with blood-red talons which could be vicious and tearing. Yes, you watch out, Rebecca — Marcia Storm'll make trouble between you and your boy as sure as my middle name's Angela!'

146

10

Marcia Hits Back

The next few days passed very swiftly, and Mike and I grew more and more fond of each other. Marcia seemed to have given it up as a bad job, for we neither saw nor heard of her, and I always tried to avoid meeting her coming in and out of Reeves's studio.

I saw quite a lot of Reeves, however, and he continued to be pleasant. Towards the end of my second week at Mrs. Tate's he met me on the stairs one day and said:

'Another day will see my portrait of Marcia finished — and then, if you have no objections Miss Kay, I'd very much like to ask Mike for his permission to have *you* sit for me.'

I said: 'Why, of course, Mr. Reeves.'

'Usual rates, of course. You *are* sure you don't mind yourself? You aren't — frightened?'

I was, but I wasn't going to show it. I laughed: 'Of course not. It must be coincidence that the other five girls who've been killed have been models of yours.'

'Perhaps it is; although personally I think that's stretching it a bit far. To me it seems there's a definite plan and motive behind the crimes. I feel certain of it.'

I smiled: 'Then I really should be afraid, shouldn't I? If I am murdered I'll come back and haunt you, Mr. Reeves.'

He shook his head: 'Please don't joke about it, Miss Kay. It isn't funny to me — everyone suspects . . . even the police are keeping a very close eye on me. I don't like being watched at any time.'

He was still frowning when I left him a few minutes later.

Mike picked me up at eight, and we went out to dine. He had chosen a quiet little place in the Village itself, where the service was poor and the only entertainment was hammered out of a battered piano by a large man, who occasionally gave tongue in a hoarse, whining voice. But the food was good, and one could enjoy a certain amount of privacy afforded by the tiny curtained alcoves.

Mike said: 'Rebecca, has Reeves asked you to pose for him?'

He was tapping the table top with his fork and staring at the red-checked cloth pattern. I nodded. 'He has, Mike. He said he'd ask if it was all right with you . . . '

'If he means are you under exclusive contract for the lousy salary I pay you, the answer is no. It'd be a leg-up for you to have your portrait done by Reeves — especially with his unusual knack of spotting outstanding poses. His work hangs permanently in the local galleries, and is also exhibited at almost every new exhibition.

'It always attracts comment. He's had a private showing of some of his work at a private gallery on Fortieth Street, and the critics all agreed that he brought something new and virile to contemporary painting. His canvases, the better ones, sell for upwards of one thousand dollars. I understand he's just disposed of the one of Mornia Garish he did for a cool one thousand five hundred, to some bigwig from Park Avenue. Yes, he'd be a useful stepping stone for you if that's what you want . . . and under ordinary circumstances I'd welcome the suggestion. But . . . you may as well know what I think, Rebecca. I told him whether or not you posed was your business. But I also told him that although you aren't in any way bound, I'm against the idea.'

'You told him that, Mike?'

'Just that. I think you know why as well as I do.'

'I think so. You mean — the other models who've been strangled? You think *I* might be?' He traced the pattern of the cloth with a stiff forefinger.

'I don't know for sure. But I don't think it's worth the risk. Because it's such a confoundedly *big* risk.'

'But if I took care to have somebody always around to see I didn't come to any harm . . . '

'Some of the other girls thought that. In fact, with one it was almost a full year before she started going out alone, or staying in by herself. She had a roommate, and the roommate arranged things so they could always be together.

'They did it for a year, never leaving each other. And then they grew careless . . . because in the meantime Reeves had had another model, and *she* hadn't been murdered either.

'They started to live their ordinary lives again. And the second time she went out alone the strangler *got her*! And the day after that *he got her successor*! Whoever commits these ghastly murders can be patient and wait, without forgetting. Five years might pass and even then you wouldn't be safe! Every girl who has posed for Reeves since he arrived here two years ago has been strangled. That is a fact no-one can avoid. And that's why I'm asking you — free agent though you are — *not* to pose for Gilbert Reeves!

'I don't know the reason for these diabolical acts,' Mike went on. 'And I expect it'd take a Sherlock Holmes to work it out, but I do believe anyone who sits for Reeves is asking for trouble . . . '

'Mike, you don't think Reeves *himself* . . . ?'

Mike shrugged: 'No more than anyone else . . . '

151

'But some of his studies are so — queer.'

He grinned at that: 'Not as queer as some of mine, I bet. So you may just as well wonder if I'm the killer.'

'I *did*. I decided you weren't.'

'Thanks. You're right, I'm not.' Mike said: 'Let's go.'

We went.

★   ★   ★

The following evening I ran full tilt into Marcia Storm as I was going in. She was leaning fully dressed in her street clothes against the door of Reeves's studio, and as I came forward she stood in the narrow hallway, directly in front of me.

I thought she meant to make trouble, and my fists clenched. I wasn't going to take any back answers from her again. I said:

'Excuse me . . . '

'Hold on, my pet. Surely you aren't walking on and cutting me dead — I *should* be hurt.'

'If you've come here to be funny . . . '

'But I haven't. Matter of fact, I've come here to apologize. You see, my sweet, I've realized you were right — I don't want Mike in the way you want him. In fact, I don't want him at all now. I have plucked myself a beautiful old gentleman with a mauve waistcoat and a cherry-red nose, and a bank balance which takes fifteen bank clerks to keep it in order. What the vulgar used to call a rich gentleman friend, or what the intelligentsia would term a 'sugar daddy.' Only the old dear is so frightfully decrepit a better term might be a sugar gran-pappy. Whichever you use, it boils down to the same thing — I'm milking him frightfully. Like my furs?'

I snapped: 'I'm sorry for him. And not interested in you. So let me pass.'

She eyed me reproachfully.

'My pet! Is this my reward for troubling to wait for you coming in? Especially to apologize?'

'I don't know what your motive is. I can't see why you feel any apology to be necessary. In any case, I don't want one.'

'But I want to make one,' she

vociferated. 'Indeed I do.'

'Why?'

She raised her eyebrows. Said: 'I suppose I'm not awfully sporting, my pet. But . . . I still like Mike, and I'm sorry I was so rude to him and you. I'm also sorry about the malicious things I've said in my temper to common acquaintances.'

'They were repeated to Mike and me,' I said witheringly. 'We simply ignored them. We guessed their origination.'

She smiled, and, looking at her, I could see it was a straightforward enough smile, without any malice in it.

Her entire attitude was one of humble apology — hard to believe, coming from Marcia, of all people. But the more I looked at her, the more I became convinced she was sincere. She went on:

'I've said and done some nasty things. I admit it. The only excuse I can give is my rotten nature. I was humiliated and angry at the time. Now I've come to my senses again, and I'd like you and Mike to know I want to be friends again, and that I'd like you both to forget and forgive, as the saying has it.'

I was taken aback. I murmured: 'But I don't . . . '

Marcia had thrust her hand out. I regarded it for a moment with mixed feelings. Certainly I didn't want to have any enemies as vicious as Marcia could be; furthermore, I thought it big of her to extend the olive branch this way. For Marcia wasn't at all the type that was given to making humble apologies. So at length I gripped her hand and shook it.

'Thanks,' she drawled. 'I knew you weren't the kind to harbor grudges. But Mike . . . '

'Mike isn't the kind either. He'll be only too happy to know you've had a change of heart.'

She nodded. 'I think he will. I'd very much like to see him and put things right. Would you mind if I saw him tonight?'

I suddenly had a fleeting doubt, said: 'Is all this simply an effort to work your way in with Mike again? If so . . . '

'It isn't. I swear it. I merely want to see him to tell him what I've told you. I want to atone for my silliness.'

'But Mike is seeing me tonight . . . ' I

155

began. 'He is calling for me about eight.'

'Then you wouldn't have any objection to my coming along here and apologizing, would you?'

I considered a moment. 'No, I don't think so. If you come about eight, will that do?'

She said: 'You're a sport, Rebecca . . . I'll be here.'

I watched her walk out and turned to go upstairs. I found Mrs. Tate regarding me from the stair top. She said: 'What was all *that* about, dearie?'

I laughed: 'It seems we were both wrong about Marcia, Mrs. Tate. She's just made a most humble apology and intends to make it to Mike as well. She was quite sincere about it. Seems to have found herself a pot of gold at the end of a man with a nose and waistcoat like a rainbow, and has decided that's a little better even than having the monopoly of a fashionable art photographer.'

Mrs. Tate sniffed; said: 'I wouldn't trust that girl any farther than I could throw Sophie Tucker, and at that I suffer from rheumatism in both shoulders. You watch your step, m'dear. I know these high-toned models with their two-faced scheming; they're the biggest bunch of hypocrites that ever lived. I'm telling you that she's probably out to get your man back again by showing him a side of her nature he hadn't expected. The contrite girl . . . the poor, downtrodden little stray who's been cast off like a patrolman's service boots at the end of a busy day. You mark what I say . . .'

'If that's her idea she's going the wrong way about it,' I said, 'because Mike won't think any more of her for latching on to some rich old fool, and anyway, he won't have anything more to do with her.'

Mrs. Tate said: 'That about the sugar daddy may be an act to rouse Mike's jealous nature. He has a jealous nature, hasn't he?'

'He has. But I don't think it would operate as far as Marcia's concerned now. I don't want to sound too sure of myself, but the truth is I'm pretty sure of Mike. I think I know him by now, and the only thing that would make him change his mind about me would be if I happened to be Marcia's type. And I don't. Therefore, if she is up to some little stunt, she's welcome. I wish her luck, but I'm afraid she won't have any.'

Mrs. Tate shook her head and wandered off to her kitchen. I went right up and started to wash and dress for going to dinner with Mike.

When I was ready in the new green, tight-fitting dress I'd bought, I sat and read *Mademoiselle* to while away the time. It was seven-thirty by my wrist watch when there was a knock on the door and I stood up expectantly and called: 'Come in.'

It wasn't Mike. It was Marcia.

She was dressed in a neat black costume and still showed a great deal of contrition in her face. She said:

'Sorry I'm a bit early, my pet. I have a date with my corpulent Cuthbert a little later on, and until then I thought we might improve the golden hour by chatting of this and that whilst we wait for the man of your heart. No objections, I suppose?'

'None. Although I don't really think it's

essential for you to apologize to Mike at all. It'll only embarrass him, and I can explain how you feel about things now.'

She waved a gloved hand languidly, said: 'I must make the *amende honorable*, my pet. Otherwise I won't have an easy conscience about things. May I deposit the body?'

I nodded to a seat and she sat down. I poured a drink for her and one for myself, handed it to her. She snapped open her cigarette case and offered it to me. I took one. She lit it for me. I passed some compliment about her hair. She passed an equally hypocritical compliment about my dress.

We sat about talking and drinking and smoking, and I began to feel a bit light-headed after a time. Things were inclined to rock uncertainly, solid things like the wardrobe and the table, and the very room. It was like being on the Ferry going to Staten Island . . .

There was a blurring sensation with it. I passed a hand across my brow and muttered: 'Rather stuffy, isn't it?'

'Horribly so,' agreed Marcia. 'Shall I

open the window?'

I said: 'Don ' — don' bother — I will — '

I lurched across the room like a ship in a high sea. I wasn't thinking straight anymore. I fumbled with the window for a minute, hurt my thumb, and said: 'T'hell. Stuck. Doesn't madder.'

I poured another drink for Marcia, but my hand shook so hard I spilt half of it. Marcia murmured: 'Here, my pet. Let me.'

I sat down and watched her; she brought the drink across, leaned over to hand it to me — and upset it all over my new dress!

'Oh!' I jumped up with an exclamation, and she heaped apology on me and recrimination upon herself.

'How frightfully clumsy of me. I *am* an idiot!'

'It's ruined,' I wailed. 'Ruined . . . and I paid so much for it . . . look at it . . . ' I felt so funny in the head that I simply sat down and began to wail.

Marcia bent over me, said: 'Hold up your arms, dear. If we get it off quickly I know a sure way of saving it. Hurry . . . '

Half-dazed, I held my arms up and she slid the dress over my head. It was cold being in just my underwear, and I shivered and said: 'I'll have to get something else on . . . '

The clock on the mantelpiece struck *eight*. Marcia said:

'I'll get it for you, darling. Where is it?'

I felt awfully hazy. My head was spinning, and for some strange reason I couldn't remember what or who Marcia was or what she was doing in the room. I felt as if I were going to droop over and sleep at any minute.

Marcia was looking out of the door. Then she glanced back at me. She said: 'Right — be quick about it!'

And then, through my whirling consciousness, I spotted three men and two girls coming in through the doorway. The girls at once threw their coats aside and adopted attitudes on the chairs and the divan. The men did likewise, and the third one came towards me, sat beside me, and put an arm about me. He gave a tug and I fell into his arms, and relaxed against his chest. I was too muddled and dreamy to try to straighten things out.

Marcia, still at the door, suddenly hissed: 'Right. Here he comes now. I'm vanishing into the bedroom . . . you know what to say, if he speaks.' She turned and hurried into the bedroom, and she had hardly gone when the outer door opened, to reveal *Mike*!

11

Address Unknown

Mike!

At the time I was too dazed to do anything to defend myself. I was really in the air, and I know just how it must have looked to him, seeing me in my underwear in the arms of another man in my own rooms, on my own settee, and with what was obviously a necking party in progress. The two liquor glasses didn't do anything to spoil the illusion, either.

I gaped at him dumbly as he stood in the doorway. His face had gone very red, and his fists were clenched. The other two couples went on shouting, laughing and yelling riotously, and the man who had hold of me kept trying to pull my face to his to kiss me.

Mike said, in a quiet voice: 'What *is* all this, Rebecca?'

The man with me looked at him and

sneered: 'Sheer off, Peeping Tom. If the little lady invites us in to a necking party, who in hell are you to come prying round?'

Mike said softly: 'Just her fiancé, Mister.'

'Yeah? Then I'm sorry for you, you poor boob. Anyway you aren't wanted round here — Rebecca's busy. Beat it.'

That was too much for Mike. He strode forward, swung, and took one sock at the man beside me. That gent suddenly went glassy-eyed, as if he'd been struck by the business end of a subway train. He was lifted right over the back of the settee and flopped on to the floor behind, using his neck as a touch-down gadget. He was out.

Mike looked at me and, hazed as I was, the scorn and contempt on his face made me feel sick. He snapped: 'Seems I did myself a bad turn throwing over Marcia for you.' He grunted: 'At least you could have spared me walking into the middle of *this*. I suppose you forgot I was coming tonight?'

'You don't unner'stan', Mike,' I mumbled,

fighting to make myself understood. 'I'm not myself . . .'

'Maybe you *are*. Maybe this is *really* yourself, and not the kid I thought I knew. Whichever way it is, I've got no use for your kind. You'd better see about teaming up with Marcia — maybe you can start a club. Call it the 'Dames who've made a sucker out of Mike Patterson club'!'

'Mike — it isn't what it seems — I *feel* funny.'

He eyed me: 'You *look* funny, too. You're a pip, Rebecca. I hadn't any idea you were inclined to this kind of game . . . glad I found out in time. Thanks for the innocent kid act you pulled. You *really* had me fooled . . . but now you don't need me anymore. You can pose for Reeves, can't you? So long.'

He turned, walked towards the door. I screamed: '*Mike!*'

I staggered up and tried to lurch after him. The door shut behind him and I flopped right down there on the floor, the whole room whirled around in front of me. I had a feeling the top half of my head was flying off, and then there was nothing but a blackout.

★　★　★

From miles and miles away I heard the voices shrieking at me in the darkness.

'Glad I found out in time — glad I found out in time — glad I found out — found out — found out — found out . . .'

And Marcia's superior tones: 'Cigarette, my pet — cigarette, my pet — cigarette — cigarette . . .'

And Mrs. Tate's: 'She's up to no good — no good — no good. Mark what I say — hypocrites — hypocrites — hypocrites!'

Then Marcia again: 'She's coming round. About time, too.'

I opened my eyes and the darkness melted, revealing me sitting propped up in my own bed. My head ached terribly and there was a dry sawdust feeling in the back of my throat. Marcia and the man who had sat with me and been knocked out by Mike were in the room. Marcia was touching my brow with a damp cloth.

The other two couples, ready to leave, were standing watching at the bedroom door.

Marcia said: 'Good morning, Rebecca. You've been out almost five hours. How do you feel, my pet?'

I struggled farther up and held my brow. I said: 'Mike — did — did he come back?'

Marcia smiled. 'I'm very much afraid this has washed you up with dear Mike. He won't come back again. How unfortunate.'

'You — ' I hissed venomously. 'Don't think you can get away with this, you cheap, lowdown skunk! You dirty sneaking harlot!'

Marcia murmured: 'My, my. Born and bred in the slums — and wouldn't you know it?'

The others grinned.

'*You* did this . . . ' I panted. '*You* fixed it all. You knew what you were going to do when you pretended to make it up with me. You had it all arranged!'

'Really? That's a wild accusation if you

like. I did nothing, my pet. How, may I ask, could I force you to go to the arms of another man?'

'You *know* how you did it,' I shrieked. 'My *drink* . . . '

'You poured the first drinks yourself, and you seemed queer even then. Besides, this party was entirely your own notion. I wasn't even anywhere *near* here. Was I, you people?'

'You weren't!' agreed the other five together.

'And didn't Miss Kay arrange the whole little shemozzle *unaided*?' insisted Marcia.

'She certainly *did*,' they nodded. 'We came here at her express invitation. And then her boyfriend comes busting in and acting as if he *owned* the place.'

'So you see, dear, in face of five witnesses there isn't a way out for you, is there now? And by tomorrow it'll be all over town just what a fool you made of Michael J. Patterson. These girls and boys will see to that.'

I sank back on the bed. It was clear now that Marcia had arranged everything;

somehow she had drugged me with something I hadn't noticed, and the drug had taken gradual effect and sapped me of my control. When she had seen Mike on the way, she had called in her friends, who had been waiting in the passage, and the stage had been rapidly set, with me too far gone to realize what they were doing to me.

But — *would Mike believe me?*

I had to *make* him! Surely he would at least give me a hearing when I was able to talk clearly! I looked at the grinning six. I said wearily: 'If you've done what you set out to do, will you get out now, please?'

Marcia smiled at me: 'Of course, my pet. You *must* be feeling rather out of condition, mustn't you, after one of your wild parties? We were just going, anyway. Only stayed to make sure you came round all right. Good night, my pet . . . '

The man who'd sat with me on the settee chuckled: 'Honey, if ever you want a steady boyfriend, just give me a ring.'

I snapped: 'If you ever come within smelling distance of me again I'll ring for the police. Get out!'

Still laughing together, they got out. I lay my head back on the pillow and tried to calm my jumping nerves to figure out just how it had been done. I couldn't. I fell asleep again.

*   *   *

'And this is the cigarette she gave you to smoke?' said Mrs. Tate the following morning.

'That's it. I found it in the ash-tray. It must have gone out half-smoked.'

She examined it, sniffed it, then lit it and took a deep draw. That done, she stubbed it out on the fireside curb and looked at it again.

'Yes, it was doped,' she nodded. 'I've come across the stuff before. It's a little known plant which grows in Cuba. They ship it here in vast quantities. There are one or two spots you can get hold of it in Greenwich Village.

'It is barely distinguishable from ordinary cigarette tobacco, but its effects are vastly different. You know; you've experienced them. It's in great demand by the wolves round this district. Very great demand.'

'Then if I tell Mike that, he'll realize how it happened?'

She pondered the question. 'Don't forget that you have five people to testify you arranged that party, will you? Mike may think you're trying to pull the wool over his eyes by claiming to be drugged when actually you were drunk.'

I said helplessly: 'Then what *can* I do, Elsie?'

'There's only one thing to do. You'll have to find some reliable witness who can testify that the job was faked.'

I shook my head: 'There isn't anyone who can!'

'There isn't? How about me? I can tell Mike I saw five people slinking about in the hall before he came, and that I saw Marcia going into your room. I can tell him about her pleading with you to let her come and apologize to him tonight, can't I?'

'You did see the five lurking in the passage, then?'

'No, dearie, I didn't see a thing. I was

in bed with my rheumatics, but if you say
that's how it was, then that's how it was,
and I don't mind telling a few lies to
square things again. I know you're telling
the truth, dearie. I can read faces, as I
told you there isn't a dishonest line in
yours, and if that lummox of yours was
any judge of character he'd have known
that party wasn't your idea. You bring him
to me and I'll see he gets told a few home
truths.'

I thanked her gratefully. Whatever
happened, I knew I could always count
on her for the best advice. Since I'd left
home I'd come to look on her almost as a
mother, and she knew it and felt flattered.
She was a lonely soul really. Her husband,
as she told it to me, had been a sea rover.
He'd roved so far one voyage that he'd
roved right out of her life and she hadn't
seen him again. Looking in a glass she
then found she'd put on weight and
was too old to marry again. She hadn't
any children, and likewise she hadn't any
money. So she'd converted the front
rooms of the house into studio premises,
and arranged the little flat on the second

floor. By letting these two she'd eked out a scanty living, but a living just the same. The reason she was always so cheerful in spite of recurrent hardships was, she said, because whenever she felt downhearted she just thought how much worse off she'd have been if her husband hadn't left her, and that always cheered her up and made her feel like bursting into song.

For all of that she had a warm and human heart, and I was inclined to think she missed the big, bluff, bearded man, of whom she had a photograph occupying an honored position over the fire. I pointed out to her once or twice that if the nail gave, the photo was likely to fall right into the flames, and at that she'd grinned and said: 'That's where the man himself'll go someday, so why worry, dearie?'

So it was with the offer of her help, and a slightly more hopeful outlook, I started for work.

I felt a little trepidation as I walked into the outer office, for I didn't quite know how Mike would receive me. As it turned out, though, he didn't receive me at all. The secretary said: 'Oh, Rebecca, Mr.

Patterson left this for you.'

I took the long envelope in surprise. I opened it, and sixteen ten-dollar bills fell out into my hand. With them was a short note:

Miss Kay,

I am called away on business for a short time, and I am taking this opportunity of dispensing with your services. In view of the happenings of last night you will readily understand this, I think.

Enclosed is a month's salary in lieu of notice.

If you are seeking fresh employment I would advise you to register with a reputable agency. The Excelsior Agency on Tenth Avenue is such, and should be able to find you suitable employment.

If references regarding your work are desired, I will supply you with same on written application.

My thanks for your cooperation during our short spell of working together.

Sincerely,

MICHAEL J. PATTERSON.

I was shocked; I stood staring at the note and the money with wide-open eyes. At last I turned to the secretary:

'Mary — where did he go?'

She shook her head: 'I haven't any idea, Rebecca. He simply came in this morning half-drunk, as if he'd been drinking all night, flung that on my desk, said he was going out of town, and told me to tell you it wouldn't be any use your trying to see him again. I'm awfully sorry.'

I bit my lip. 'It's all right, Mary. We had a bit of a misunderstanding and he couldn't see beyond his own silly nose.'

'Most men are like that. He'll come round.'

I nodded and walked slowly from the office. I went down into the street and flagged a passing taxi. I said: 'Dexter Gardens, and please hurry, driver.'

As we bowled along, the driver said: 'I seen you in *Strange Worlds Magazine*, lady.'

'You did?'

'I sure did,' he chuckled. 'Lyin' in a coffin without a fig leaf to your name. *Wow!* Brother! Was dat sumpin'?'

I didn't answer. He went on: 'I get

Strange Worlds every week, you see. Lookin'
forward to seein' a whole lot more of you.'

I said, without interest: 'How'd you
know it was me?'

'Well, you look like the dame and you
come out of Mike Patterson's office once
or twice. I circulate round that district
and I get to know his models. Picked
Mister Patterson himself up earlier.'

I leaned forward: 'You did? Where did
you drive him to?'

'Same address you gave, Dexter Gardens. That's where he has his hang-out,
ain't it?'

'Yes. That's it. Did he — did he leave
again?'

'I don't know, lady. He looked to me
like he was too drunk to see straight, but
he didn't ask me to wait. I drove right off
after I'd seen him safely inside.'

I sat up with renewed hope. I
murmured: 'Then I may catch him after
all. Can you go any faster?'

He stepped on it, and we shot through
the traffic, under the officious noses of
traffic cops. The taxi drew up in front
of Dexter Gardens apartment building,

and I jumped out. I said to the cabby: 'You can wait.'

He waited. I almost raced into the vestibule and grabbed hold of the janitor, who was seated in his little office reading a paper. I said: 'Mr. Patterson . . . is he in?'

The janitor folded his paper in a leisurely manner, drawled:

'Who wants to see him?'

'Oh, don't you remember me? I've been here with him once or twice. I'm his model — Miss Kay.'

'That's right, so you are, Miss. Mr. Patterson gave me orders not to say where he'd gone, Miss.'

'Then he *has* gone?' I echoed.

'Left a few minutes back. Gave me orders not to say where he was headin'. Gave me *ten bucks* to make sure . . . ' he hinted.

I opened my bag and took out twenty dollars. I thrust them into his hands: 'Where has he gone? Quickly.'

'Los Angeles. I called a cab to take him to the airport, and looked out the time of the planes.'

'Which airport?' I demanded, feeling

like shaking him. 'And what time does his plane leave?'

'La Guardia Airport, and eleven-thirty if it's on schedule.'

I started to leave, then paused: 'Did he say which part of Los Angeles he was going to?'

The janitor shook his hoary head: 'Nope.'

I raced back to the taxi. If Mike got away there was no saying when I'd see him again. There was also the likelihood that he would go on a stupendous 'bender,' trying to forget the raw deal he thought he'd had from me.

The cabby stepped on it through town, and before long the airport loomed into view. I jumped from the cab and ran through the terminal and up to the information desk. The trim blonde behind the counter simply shook her head, said: 'If you wanted the Pan Am flight to Los Angeles, you've had it, lady. She's taking off the runway *now*!'

The last hope of immediate reconciliation was gone on the wings of that transcontinental flight.

12

Not that Kind of Work!

The whole of that day and the day following I did nothing except ring up the office and try to find out if Mike had been in touch with his secretary. Whether she was fooling me or not I couldn't be certain, but she denied having heard from him.

So that left me stumped. If I'd known where he was I think I'd have squandered every dollar I had to get a plane ticket and go down to him, then and there. But it wasn't much use going to Los Angeles and trusting to luck to find Mike.

So I moped.

Three days crawled by like three centuries.

And then I began to realize that if I wanted to live I'd have to get work. I couldn't take it easy, upset or not. I took Mike's letter from my bag and glanced at it. Then I put my gladdest rags on, made sure not a hair on my head was out of place, that the seams of my stockings ran straight and true up the roundness of the back of my legs, and that my nails were immaculate. Mike had often said: 'The first thing us guys look at on a prospective model is hair, stocking seams, and nails. That's the three biggest points. Get careless on one of them and you wash your chances out pronto, no matter what your other talents.'

I had coffee on the fourth morning in Mrs. Tate's kitchen before I started out. She was almost as upset as I was about the way things had gone haywire.

'The big heel,' she sniffed. 'Why in heck'd he want to go bouncing off like that for? Couldn't he even give you a chance to explain things?'

'I suppose he thought there wasn't anything to explain and decided to get out of it for a time until he felt better . . . '

She grumbled: 'That's the trouble with men. If they think a woman's stood them up they get that touchy you wouldn't know it! They fly off the handle at the first

180

crack out of the box, and they act like big spoilt kids who can't get their own way. They get tied to a woman and work her half to death, let her live what bit of life she's got bearing their brats and washing their socks, and cooking their food, then expect *her* to look up to them as the great provider! Great provider baloney. If they could see themselves coming in from work, yanking their shoes off and toasting their corns at the fire while the wife gets hot food on the table, then sitting down and eating in shirt sleeves and dirty boiler suits, making noises like a pig, they'd get a shock. And that's what a *woman* has to put up with!'

I smiled: 'Oh, it isn't all that bad, Mrs. Tate — '

'Mine was,' she grunted. 'In fact, from the third day of our honeymoon all I was thinking about was how soon he'd get another ship and beat it. It couldn't have been too soon for my liking. I remember the day — four weeks after we'd got hitched — that he came in and said: 'I got meself a ship, Elsie. Sailin' day after tomorrow.' I never helped pack any bag so gladly as I helped pack his seabag.'

She looked at the photograph above the fire: 'Sea Dogs! Yep, that just about sums them up. Or *him*, at any rate. Sea *dogs*!'

I smiled: 'I think you'd still welcome him if he blew in out of the blue tomorrow.'

She opened her mouth to protest, looked at me, then shut it again. She looked at the picture, then said: 'I reckon you're right, honey. A woman gets kind of lonesome without a man. I like to hear the sound of a man's voice, laying down the law, and telling his family how *he'd* go about saving the world if *he* was President. There's even something attractive in hearing them snoring like hogs in bed beside you . . . yes, I guess I'd take him back — but he won't come. I know him.'

She was holding the picture in her hands and smiling when I finally left her.

Reeves came jumping from his studio as I walked by, laid a hand on my arm.

'I was waiting for you.'

'For me, Mr. Reeves? Why?'

'I heard what happened. About the

party. I could have told you Mike isn't an understanding man when it comes to necking sessions. He's a jealous man, Miss Kay, always has been.'

I stared at him: 'I expect you've heard all about how I came to invite three men and two girls to my rooms, have you? And how Mike walked in and found out about my duplicity.'

'It does get round.'

'It certainly *does*. But you've got the wrong version. Do you think for a second — even if I were that type of woman — that I'd arrange such a party, *knowing that Mike was calling for me*? Surely you don't think I'm *that* dumb?'

He looked puzzled: 'Then it *didn't* happen?'

'It happened all right. But I had nothing to do with it. Not a thing. It was entirely Marcia's idea. I'd like to kill that dirty sneaking . . . well, you know what. She fixed the whole thing by doping me.'

His face changed. He said: 'Now, why didn't I think of that! Naturally, that would be the way it was. Marcia threatened once or twice during her sittings to get even with you and Mike. So she did manage it, after all!'

'She did. But she won't get any satisfaction from it. The minute I find out where Mike is he gets the facts. I have reliable witnesses to prove Marcia had those 'guests' planted.'

'But where is Mike? Why haven't you told him before about this?'

I shrugged: 'He left town. He should be somewhere in Los Angeles by now. I was too late to catch him before he went.'

'Then you aren't working for him anymore? At least, not until he returns?'

'Perhaps not even then,' I murmured. 'He left me a note which indicated pretty clearly that he considered our relationships, both business and personal, were at an end. He advised me to get in touch with a model agency.'

Reeves smiled: 'You don't need to do that, Miss Kay. My offer to have you pose for me still goes. Now there isn't anything to prevent you. Mike was against the idea of course. I expect he told you that?'

'Only because he was afraid for my safety.'

'You'll be safe. And it will save you a great deal of wasted time and worry. The agencies are overcrowded, you know, they haven't even got jobs for their regular models.'

For a moment I was inclined to take his offer, but prudence held me from accepting. Mike had said *no*, and if I hoped to square things with him it wasn't a very good idea to go doing something he'd expressly warned me against. I shook my head politely but firmly, said: 'I'm awfully grateful, but I couldn't accept, Mr. Reeves. I don't want to antagonize Mike any more than I can help.'

Reeves said: 'But Mike doesn't care about you now.'

'Not now. But he'll realize how wrong he's been when I get the chance to put matters right. Until then I'm following his advice. If he'd thought I should pose for you I expect he'd have said so in his letter.'

Reeves smiled: 'As you say. I think you're being silly, but . . . I know it isn't any use trying to dissuade you. I can't understand what power that Mike of

185

yours has over beautiful girls like you. Why do you humble yourself so much for him?'

'It isn't a question of humbling myself,' I flushed. 'It's just that I can't blame Mike for thinking what he did, and I don't mean to give him up simply because he's jumped to a conclusion. If an explanation will set things right, he'll have it.

'It isn't as if he didn't care for me any longer. I'm sure he still loves me just as much, but he feels hurt and upset, and feels that Fate keeps giving him nasty kicks in the pants.'

Reeves spread his hands and smiled: 'No sense in giving you an argument, I can see. Ah, well, if you find you can do with a job don't hesitate to call and see me. I'm doing a bit of scenic work for a railway company, to make ends meet until I find another suitable model. I'm a little tired of Marcia — want someone younger and fresher. I can't portray anyone adequately if I don't admire them.'

'Thanks, Mr. Reeves, I'll remember that.'

The agency offices were on the sixteenth floor of a large and modern building. They were quiet, well-appointed, and besides myself contained one or two other models, both men and women.

The trim secretary switched on the intercom when I gave her my name and said into it: 'A Miss Kay to see you, sir.'

'About what?' came the thin, metallic voice.

'With a view to being placed on our lists.'

'Send her in.'

I went into the inner office and confronted the brains of the agency. He was a fat and florid man, bulging over the sides of the office chair he sat in, and sporting a collection of double chins and a white carnation. Despite his circumference there was a great deal about him which looked sinister to my gaze — the shiftiness of his eyes, the whiteness of his hands, the cruel gash which was his mouth. I expect he was actually quite a respectable business man, probably a good father and husband, and scrupulously fair in his dealings, but sinister was the way he struck me, and I felt an immediate dislike for him.

I didn't show it.

He was speaking in a clipped voice into a phone: 'Yes, we can let you have a couple of models for the before and after taking Bildup Pills ad. Send them over right away . . . yes. Fine. Good day.'

★   ★   ★

It was an act; that was obvious by the fact that none of the outbound lines were lit on his phone. It was an act calculated to impress me with the extent of business. He slammed the phone down, said: 'Miss Kay, isn't it? You wished to see me, I think — I'm very busy at the moment, a very busy man indeed, so if you'll just give me a few particulars of yourself, the type of work you do, the people you've worked for, and the rates you expect, I'll see if I can do anything for you within the next few days, oh, and by the way, our commission is ten per cent for each sitting we secure for you; is that quite agreeable to you?'

He said this all in one breath, leaving me feeling quite weak, then regarded me keenly.

'I haven't been a model for very long,' I confessed. 'In fact, I'll be honest and admit to only having had a few weeks' experience.'

His face changed; he said: 'In that case, Miss Kay, I'm sorry. We only accept experienced models for registration here.'

'But I was advised to come to you by my former employer.'

'Your former employer? Who was that?'

'Michael J. Patterson,' I murmured, not feeling very hopeful.

The change was astonishing. '*Mike*? Why, you should have told me that before. So you worked for Mike, did you? Hmm. That's a strong recommendation in itself. What type work did you do? The usual nude studies?'

'Pretty nearly everything,' I told him. 'Nude, cover shots, a little advertising work . . . whatever Mike wanted me to do.'

He nodded: 'Stand up and walk across the room. Yes — yes. Can you show me

189

any samples of your work?'

I delved into my handbag and offered him one or two glossies. He glanced over them and gave me an encouraging smile.

'Very well, Miss Kay. I'll put these on file, and take further details. Would you have any objection to posing for art classes, of both sexes?'

'I — well, I'd prefer something a little more private, if you know what I mean.'

'I think I do. And art classes pay comparatively little for their models. Very well. I'll see what I can get you. I have your address and telephone number. If anything turns up I'll get in touch with you at once. Good day.'

'Thank you.'

I left. It seemed to me that there hadn't been a lot of hope in his voice when I had left him. Perhaps Reeves was right and there was a shortage of work for regular models, let alone rank amateurs like myself.

Later that day I telephoned Mike's studio. I got the same answer. No address, no message. No, he hadn't communicated.

The following afternoon Mrs. Tate came bounding upstairs to tell me someone wanted me on the phone in the hall. I thought of Mike at first, and rushed down, but sane reasoning told me not to be too hopeful, and it was lucky I wasn't or I might have built myself up for a big let-down.

It was the agency.

'Miss Kay? There is a call for a model here which may be of some interest to you. Five foot eight, well formed, about eighteen. Nude studies. Private artist's home at Staten Island. Report immediately. Usual rates. Would that be suitable for you?'

'For how long?'

'Three or four days, possibly more. We just had the request phoned in by the artist's manservant.'

'It sounds fine; yes, I'll go along.'

'The address is Coronado, Fletcher Mansions, Staten Island. Ask for Mister Pidgeon.'

I went back upstairs and put on my

best again. I wondered how I was going to feel posing for someone other than Mike. I decided it didn't matter how I felt, I had to live, and I might as well either get used to it or get back to the sweatshop. So I went.

Coronado, the mansion named, was quite an imposing place. It lay in about eight acres of ground, well back from the sea front, and was constructed in that yellow brick, angular modern manner. It impressed me as being the residence of a wealthy artist, and I told myself I couldn't have any pleasanter surroundings in which to work.

I rang at bell and a small, jolly-featured fat man opened the door.

'I'm from the model agency,' I explained. 'Mr. Pidgeon needed a model . . .'

'Yes, Missy. That's me. Please do follow me!'

I followed him down a wide hall, through a small and very spotless kitchen, into a neat, round conservatory. Here were set out easels, brushes and canvases, as yet unused. The setting felt wrong. Very wrong.

'I understand you're going to do undraped studies?' I said, steeling myself.

'Undra — er — er — yes. Yes, of course. I — ha ha — I think that's the — er — general idea. Eh?'

I said: 'Since you're the artist that's up to you. Do you wish to start at once?'

'Eh? Oh, certainly. Yes. Why not, eh?'

'Then hadn't you better set your canvas?' I pointed out with a smile. He seemed nonplussed.

'My — er — canvas ... Er — of course. Yes, of course.'

He fumbled about pinning a canvas into position. All his equipment, I noticed, was new. Furthermore, he seemed to have no idea of how to go about the job. I said: 'Have you a screen?'

'A screen?' he asked, puzzled.

'For me to undress behind,' I told him, gazing closely at him.

'Oh! Why — er — I see. Suppose you use the — the room just off the hall? You'll be perfectly all right there.'

I was definitely uneasy now, but went along to the room he had indicated. I had brought my own dressing gown, and when I had donned it I returned to the studio.

He hadn't moved, and he seemed more ill at ease than ever. I said: 'Had you any particular pose in mind?'

'Er — I — I think I'll leave that to you.'

I discarded the gown and struck a pose, standing on the scrap of velvet which seemed to be there for the purpose. He said: 'That's excellent, my dear — excellent. Just hold that.' He picked up a piece of charcoal and made several passes at the canvas. But he wasn't looking at the canvas! His eyes were busy elsewhere . . .

I suddenly bent, picked up the gown, draped it on myself again, and walked over. The marks he had made on the canvas betrayed him.

13

Murder!

I knew at once that what I had suspected all along had turned out to be absolutely true. I taxed the little man directly with it: 'You aren't a *regular* artist, are you? You aren't even an *amateur*?'

He looked uncomfortable for a moment. 'What — er — what makes you think that?'

I indicated the canvas. 'That. No artist sketches in his complete background before determining the position of his central figure! How are you going to get me in over that without making an awful mess of your work? And if you are only doing background work, why bother to have me posing at all right now?'

He opened his hands and tried a feeble smile. 'I admit I'm just a beginner.'

'That's easily seen. But a beginner at — *what*? Not art, I'm sure.'

'But — but what else?' he protested.

'Frankly I wouldn't like to tell you. I think your motives for posing as an artist and hiring a model are not very nice.'

'Oh, I say now . . . '

'It's the truth, though, *isn't it*?'

He seemed to debate the question with himself. Then he stole a sideways glance at me. I don't know what he thought he read in my face, but whatever it was it couldn't have been right. For he said, apologetically: 'Well, since you seem to have made a very good guess I admit it wasn't *entirely* for posing I wanted a model. In fact, I rather thought we could have a bite to eat afterwards and — er — perhaps attend a show. I'm rather a lonely man.'

'I don't wonder. I detest your kind. Anyway, I'm not the girl you want — '

'But you *are* . . . '

I said contemptuously: 'I'm not the girl you're going to *get*. You've got off the bus at the wrong stop. You can pay me the fee for one hour of my time and I'll leave.'

'There isn't any reason to be annoyed about it,' he whimpered. 'If you're a good

196

girl I'll see you're treated right. I don't mind how much money I spend on a girl I like.'

I said: 'The only money I want off you is one hour's posing fee and my fares here and back. Personally I think you're a mental case.'

I turned round and walked out on him. I went into the small room I had used and began to dress. I could hear his footsteps along the passage after a time, and there wasn't any key in the door to lock it. I picked up a large piece of china plate from a handy sideboard, poised it, and waited. His steps halted outside the door. 'Listen, my dear . . . '

'If you dare to come in here you'll be sorry.'

'Oh, come now. Let's — er — not be — silly.'

He opened the door and popped his head round.

I hit him with the china plate!

His head went back again like a tortoise withdrawing into its shell. His steps retreated. I went on dressing, and when I was all through I went out into the hall.

He wasn't standing there, holding some money in his hands. Instead, a fat envelope reposed on a table by the door, with a note scrawled upon it. It said: *I'm so sorry about the misunderstanding. Please accept the requested fee, and please say nothing about the matter.*

I peeled the wad of dollars from the envelope and put it in my bag. I hollered back down the hallway: 'Since you haven't the nerve to face me yourself, hear this! I certainly *won't* keep quiet. Your kind are a menace. I'll do my level best to warn as many models as I can about you, and as many agencies.'

Then I walked out.

I hit a payphone by the ferry and plugged a nickel into the box. I got through to the agency. I said: 'About that address you sent me along to — the guy isn't any artist; he's an old roué. He doesn't want a model; he wants a cheap woman. I walked out on him.'

'You did right. I'm sorry we sent you along there if it's as you say. Thanks for the tip — we'll write him a warning letter.'

I hung up and, feeling much better, I took the boat back. When I reached the mainland I decided to look in on Mike's office and see if anything had been heard from him. The answer was the same as usual. Nothing.

I was afraid of going to an agency again now. I had come out of that scrape all right, but only because the man was a little meek type; the henpecked husband kind who can be bawled out by a woman and made to feel ashamed any time they're being naughty boys. But next time — *next time* it might be *different*. I might not be so *lucky* next time.

I started to think about Reeve's offer, and the more I thought the more I was tempted. By the time I had reached home I had made up my mind to accept right away. Accordingly I knocked at the studio door and went in in answer to his invitation.

He was working on a poster design, depicting the sunny shores of California, and he gave me a pleasant nod.

'Mr. Reeves,' I told him, 'I've had a rather unnerving experience today.'

'I'm sorry. Anything I can do about it?'

'I don't think so. But I don't deny it's given me a shock. I never expected — well, briefly, I was hired out by the agency to a gentleman whose interest lay more in flesh and blood than in the canvas he was supposed to be working on.'

'I understand. There are many people of that nature in America, and for that matter all over the world. You didn't come to any harm, I hope?'

'Thank you, no. But I realized it's a risky business working through an agency, even a reputable one. So . . . if you still wish me to pose for you, I'll be glad to.'

'That's great,' he said enthusiastically. 'Simply wonderful. When can we start?'

'That's up to you entirely.'

'Tomorrow?'

'Why not? What time shall I come down?'

He considered. 'Say about ten? I'll rush this poster work through and we can get an early start. You won't, of course, leave me in the middle of the painting when your friend Mike comes back, will you?'

'Of course I won't. I have some principles. Thanks, Mr. Reeves.'

I left him then and walked down to the kitchen. I sat talking to Elsie for a time. She aired her views on the amorous Mr. Pidgeon in no uncertain terms, and started on another harangue about men being worms, and snakes in the grass, and such.

I went to bed early and dreamed about Mike.

* * *

I began posing for Reeves the following day. He was charming, if a slow worker, and I really enjoyed his company whilst he 'got' me on to canvas. He had travelled a great deal, and talked of strange countries and even stranger customs, and I think if I hadn't been so fond of Mike I could have fallen for him with a loud bang. But Mike was at the back of my mind during the days that followed, more and more.

Until Reeves suddenly said one morning: 'Mike's back in town.'

I came out of my pose with a jump, said eagerly: 'He *is*? *Where*? When did he get back? Where's he been?'

Reeves shook his head. 'He isn't saying. He seems a bit subdued, poor chap. I haven't seen him myself, but so Orvel Barrat, the ham actor, tells me. I know he's moved his studio and his apartment, and no one seems to know just where he's moved to, although Barrat thinks he's come down into the Village itself.'

'Then — you don't know where I can get in touch with him?'

'I think I do, rather. Barrat says that Blossom Pennant is giving a little party for him tonight, with just a few guests. Mike, and Orvel himself, Harper — you remember him? — and me. I had a letter from Blossom asking me to slip round there tonight, but not actually stating what for. Blossom invites me to all her parties. I can't think why, I don't really enjoy them. But I hate to refuse her, because she once lent me a considerable sum of money when I was in a jam.'

'But — *I* haven't been asked to go!'

'My dear thing, don't worry your head

about that. Blossom's place is open house. Everybody who hears about it will be going. Why not you? And if you'll bring your witness along with you I'll make it my business to see Mike gives you a hearing.'

I said: 'Thanks, Gil. I'll do that. Are you sure Mike will go?'

'Positive. He may not want to, but he's far too polite to turn down an invitation to a little social gathering which someone has been kind enough to arrange especially for him. Yes, he'll go.'

And at that we left it.

I told Mrs. Tate about it at lunch time, and she expressed her willingness to do all she possibly could to help me. So at seven-fifteen we started out, me looking my best and Mrs. Tate arrayed in a surprisingly youthful creation which made her look half her age. It was the first time she'd been to one of what she called 'those wild orgies,' and I didn't like to disillusion her about it. This one, she was convinced, was going to be very wild, merely by the fact that it was being thrown at Blossom Pennant's. She had heard of Blossom and the carryings on at her studio blowouts.

The nearer to Blossom's we got, the more worried and nervous I became. Wondering if Mike would be there, how it would be to see him again, if he had, perhaps, forgotten me after all, or at least fallen out of love with me. Would he take the explanation, even with Mrs. Tate throwing her weight in on my side? I could only hope he would.

Mike *was* there, together with the few other guests Reeves had mentioned. It was obvious at once that Reeves had been talking to him about things, for the moment I came in he walked across and drew me aside.

'Hello, Rebecca.' His voice was low and uncertain. I said:

'I'm glad you're back, Mike — I'd like you to know just what happened that night — the full story — ' and then I started telling him, getting it off my mind with a rush, and not embroidering the case, but simply stating things as they had happened. When I was through he took my hands between his and, oblivious of the others, who were drinking and joking round the piano with Blossom, he said: 'I've been mad. I was sorry about acting as I did the minute I'd got aboard that plane. I wondered all the time if there *could* be some explanation . . . can you forgive me, Rebecca?'

'Forgive you?' I laughed. 'I never blamed you, Mike. There isn't anything to forgive.'

'There is; I should have waited for an explanation at the time. I rushed away like a hurt child.'

'Then you believe me? You don't want to speak to Mrs. Tate to hear her verify the story?'

'Of course I don't. I remember, now you've mentioned Marcia's part in it all; I remember noticing that the man who had hold of you was a particular crony of hers not long ago. But don't worry — I'll be going over to see Miss Storm later tonight, when this little gathering splits up, and then *I'll* have a few things to say to her. Not very pleasant things, either!'

'No, Mike, don't cause any more trouble.'

'There won't be any trouble. I shall

simply tell her that if she tries to interfere in my business again I'll do something very drastic about her.'

Blossom Pennant drawled from behind: 'Gettin' excited, Mike?'

'I am,' grunted Mike. 'Wouldn't you be yourself if you were made a fool of by Marcia Storm? She might have ruined my life if Rebecca hadn't been so loyal. Whatever I thought about Rebecca, I knew all the time I wasn't going to be able to stop loving her.'

Blossom laughed, in her deep tones. 'Yes, Marcia is quite a little devil, isn't she? I can't say I've a great deal of affection for her myself.'

The conversation became general after that, and Mrs. Tate prevailed upon us all to listen to her singing 'Three O'clock in the Morning.'

But I had been studying Mike's features, and what I saw there upset me. He seemed to have passed the matter of Marcia's little scheme off lightly, but I could tell by the grim set of his face that he was feeling very bitter about it.

He blamed himself for being taken in

so easily, and he looked as if he was determined to give Marcia a nasty time about it.

When the party broke up and Blossom saw us off the premises, acknowledging our thanks with a tug at her upper lip and a tilt of her monocle, Mike said: 'Here's where I go, Rebecca. I'll call round to see you after I've enjoyed my little chat with Marcia.'

'No, Mike, don't go. Leave her alone now — what does it matter what she did if she didn't succeed?'

He shook his head abruptly: 'No woman is going to pull a trick of that kind on me and get away with it,' he said. 'I won't stay long — just long enough to tell her what will happen to her if she tries to split us up again.'

'Mike . . . '

Mrs. Tate said: 'Why don't you two go in the corner coffee house and have a talk? I'll go on home and leave you to yourselves. You must have a lot to say to each other.'

Mike hesitated.

'Yes, Mike, please let's.'

At length he agreed, and we went in minus Mrs. Tate, and ordered coffee. We sat and drank it and talked for fifteen minutes, and at last Mike rose, said: 'I must go over and see Marcia. I want to get it off my chest.'

'Anyone would think you were more interested in Marcia than you are in me,' I pouted.

He kissed me, smiled, and said: 'Don't be crazy. Look here, come with me if you want to.'

'I'll take you up on that, Mike.'

'But you'll have to hang on outside,' he told me. 'What I have to say to that female Machiavelli isn't fit for your dainty little ears.'

'All right, Mike. I'll wait outside.'

We walked over to the place where Marcia had rooms. It was an unpretentious building of four floors and a basement, with a small entrance hall and a wide flight of circular stairs leading upwards. Marcia had rooms on the third floor, and Mike left me in the hall, telling me to wait a few minutes. Then he went quickly up the stairs, and I heard his footsteps dying away.

No sooner had the last step faded than a car screeched up to the door, four uniformed patrolmen fell out, and came dashing into the building. One of them snapped 'third floor' to the other three, and they raced up the stairs, not even seeing me as I stood in the shadows.

I was alarmed; what had they wanted on the third floor? Only Marcia had rooms on that floor, so it must be something connected with her, I knew. But — why the hurry? Why had they looked so excited?

I decided there was only one way to find out. I started hurrying upstairs myself, desperately afraid, and with a feeling something was very wrong.

I reached the third floor. The patrolmen were not to be seen. At the end of the passage was a partly opened door with a light streaming from it. I went rapidly along there, peered cautiously round . . .

The scene in the room made me feel sick with horror.

Mike was standing dazedly in the grip of two of the officers. The other two were standing over the bed — the room was the bedroom apparently — on which lay something with silk-clad legs and a flimsy negligee. Something which was sprawled grotesquely out, one white arm hanging limply from the bedside, one shapely leg bent up in the air, the other stretched full length towards the bedrail.

I couldn't see the face until I rushed in, frantic with anxiety.

As I entered the two officers rose from their grisly examination.

One of them said: 'Dead! Strangled the same way those other five were!'

As I saw the face, I screamed. It was Marcia Storm.

The patrolmen stared at me; one barked: 'Get out of here, lady. This isn't any place for dames . . . '

I glanced towards Mike, and they noticed the glance.

One of them said: 'Are you along with this guy?'

'I — yes, I am. But — who did it?'

Mike said: 'She was that way when I got up here. I was just taking a look at her when these idiots barged in and snapped handcuffs on me.'

I stared unbelievingly. 'He couldn't have done it,' I cried, wildly. 'We only just arrived before yourselves. He hadn't been up here more than a minute or so when you came . . . '

One of them said: 'That makes it *worse* — the body is still *warm*!'

14

Next in Line

Things looked very black for Mike.

It seemed the cops had dashed in just as he was bending over the corpse on the bed, and naturally, since the body was still warm, they could think only one thing. By the time the divisional surgeon arrived it was hard for him to state the exact time of death — he could only hazard a guess within ten minutes either way.

The precinct station, it seemed, had had a phone call only a few minutes before they had arrived on the scene. A man's voice had stated that Mike Patterson had gone over to Marcia Storm's place with the avowed intention of killing her for the filthy trick she'd played on him. Oh, yes, the motive was strong enough — and often in the past Mike had said he'd have liked to kill

Mornia Garish — so that gave him a motive for the *last* murder also.

For one horrible moment I had my own doubts; but a look from Mike's calm, level eyes told me he was telling the truth when he said he found Marcia that way.

We managed to snatch a word or two together before they took him down to book him in. He said:

'I didn't do this Rebecca. But it was done by someone who knew I meant to come over here — whoever killed Marcia was at Blossom's. They waited until the party split up, and kept their eyes on me, then hurried over to Marcia's place, dropped casually in on her as they did the other five times, and at the first opportunity strangled her. The police say that she put up a tremendous struggle for life, but whoever perpetrated this crime must have been far stronger than she was. Having done the job they slipped out again and waited in concealment until they saw us hurrying into the place. Then they put through a call to the station and told the cops to get down here.'

'But what can I *do*, Mike?'

He shook his head. 'Nothing except keep your eyes and ears open. You see, darling, now you're posing for Reeves you're logically the *next in line*!'

Then they took him away from me, and allowed me to go home with a warning that I'd better be careful as I was implicated to a certain extent.

But my mind was busy all that night and by the time day dawned I had decided to do a little private investigating off my own bat. Consequently, I turned up at Reeve's studio to continue with the pose the next morning.

He seemed surprised to see me: he had heard about the murder and had thought I wouldn't be turning in. But he set the work up, and I took the pose.

'I can't understand it,' he told me, shaking his head, 'why is it only girls who've posed for me? What's behind it? Who could have a motive for murdering every model I select?'

'I can't understand that myself. If someone objects to the girls who pose for you, why don't they murder them *before* you've completed your picture?'

'That's never happened. It's always after the picture's done. Usually about three or four days after.'

'After the last sitting?' I enquired.

He shook his head. 'No. After I've had my friends in to see the work. The minute I've touched up the canvas and it's ready for sale, I usually call in a few friends to pass opinions on it. Orvel Barrat, Harper, Culbert, and Blossom Pennant.'

I was struck by another thought: 'What's happened to the paintings of all those dead girls?'

He scratched his chin: 'Funny you should ask that. As it happens, they were all purchased by the same person . . . '

I lost my position in my eagerness: 'Who was it?'

He smiled: 'I don't think there's anything behind it of course, at least, nothing more than morbid tastes.'

He told me who the purchaser was.

I said: 'And — and the murders all take place *after* you've completed the paintings?'

'After I've *shown* them, yes.'

'Gil, just how long will it take you to

complete this one of me?'

'About three weeks, Rebecca. Why?'

'Can't you — can't you speed it up at all?'

He reflected: 'But . . . '

'I'll tell you why, Gil. If you finish this picture and show it that will put me in line for being strangled. Isn't that so? I'm pretty sure I know now who the murderer is, and I have a plan that will provide absolute proof — but I'll need your help to pull it off! You do have a gun, I suppose?'

His jaw dropped. 'Yes, I have two guns, as it happens . . . But who is the killer? And what's this plan?'

After I'd told him, he gripped my shoulders. His face pale with worry. 'My God, I believe you're right . . . But your scheme is too dangerous! Why not call in the police instead?'

I smiled faintly. 'Do you think the police would believe me? They'd think I was just trying to get Mike off the hook! And even if they *did* believe me, they'd probably never allow me to risk going through with it. But, don't you see — my

216

plan is the *only* way to ensure that Mike is completely exonerated!'

I could see that he was wavering. 'Explain your plan again.'

I ran through the details once more. 'When the painting is completed and has been shown I'll deliberately seclude myself, expose myself to danger. I feel pretty sure the strangler is unbalanced mentally; I feel sure they won't miss any opportunity to get at me, and if they do get at me that will clear Mike!'

'But, damn it all, Rebecca, you can't risk a thing like that! What if you get strangled yourself?'

'I've already told you how that won't happen — you'll have followed right behind with your gun! As soon as I'm threatened you'll burst into my room and save me. Then I can ring for the police.'

He was still doubtful. 'Look,' I said, 'you can give me your other gun, which I'll have close to hand, just in case . . . '

He considered for a moment, finally nodded: 'Very well. If you think you can clear Mike by that method, I'll cooperate. It's well worth a try, anyway. I can have this painting finished within two days if I rush it. It'll mean hard work and posing late for you, but if that's what you want, why not?'

It was agreed that we should work all out until the thing was finished and shown privately to Gil's friends. We did. I posed until I was aching and weary and almost paralyzed by maintaining the position. I posed until my head drooped, and I fell asleep through sheer tiredness. And all the time Gil worked on, bringing up a tremendous reserve of energy from somewhere, hardly eating or sleeping, simply working, working to get the portrait finished and shown.

At last it was done, and he sent a number of cards through the mail to the little party he always called in on such occasions. They arrived the following day at the time he had appointed.

They studied the nude painting of me.

'It's good — awfully good,' said Harper with enthusiasm. It's your best work yet, Gil.'

'I don't know,' put in Culbert, the cartoonist, slowly. 'To me it seems to be rather — hurried. You don't mind my being frank, do you, Gil?'

'Not at all,' Gil replied politely. 'What do you think, Blossom?'

Blossom studied it, said: 'It *is* good . . . just like all the others.'

Gil turned to Orvel Barrat, said: 'You haven't much to say. What do *you* think?'

He grunted: 'I think it's disgusting!'

'What?'

'Positively foul — it fills me with a loathly contempt for the intellect of the instigator . . . '

'That's a bit hard, Barrat. You wouldn't go that far, surely?'

'And why not, pray? How could anyone have any respect for the limited intelligence of a man who offers Orvel Barrat, the great idol of the masses, a job as the hind legs of a horse in burlesque? I tell you I won't stand for it much longer — I shall request a promotion — I shall state emphatically that unless I am elevated to the front portion of the animal they can have my resignation, forsooth!'

Reeves laughed: 'I was asking what you thought of my portrait, Barrat. Not your present position as the brainless half of a quadruped. What do you think?'

'Eh? Oh, your painting! Yes . . . hmm! I — er — delightful. Magnificent. Stupendous. Er — which one is it?'

'The one on the easel,' grunted Gil.

Orvel studied it closely through his pince-nez: 'Why, it's Rebecca. Charming. What's the meaning of the python coiled about her?'

'Innocence caught in the coils of the snake,' explained Gil. 'I'm calling it simply 'Eve','

'It's been done,' said Harper.

'I know,' Gil murmured complacently. 'But not this well!'

The gathering broke up shortly afterwards, and the guests drifted out one by one. Before they went Blossom said: 'I'm holding an informal little party tomorrow night. Perhaps you'd all like to come along?'

Gil said: 'I shall be rather busy . . . '

'Oh, come, Gil, you aren't going to disappoint me, are you?'

Gil hesitated, then said: 'Well, all right. I'll hop along, Blossom.'

Blossom turned to go, and I spoke my piece: 'I'm afraid I won't be able to get along,' I told her.

She paused, turned: 'Why not, my dear?'

'Mike — you know how it is. I must admit I don't feel very much like attending parties with Mike where he is. I'd only be a wet blanket, wouldn't I?'

She nodded: 'Very well, Rebecca. If you don't feel up to it.'

'I'll probably sit in with some improving book,' I told her. 'Spend a nice quiet evening at home for a change. I'll have plenty of peace and quietness.'

'That *will* be nice for you,' Blossom said. 'I know just how you must feel about Mike.'

They left then, and I stared at Reeves, and he stared back at me.

'By God,' he exclaimed, 'it seems like it!'

'It *is* it,' I told him. 'The farther I go, the more certain I become that I'm right . . . Anyway, we should see tomorrow night!'

15

The Trap

Reeves came up to see me the following night before he left for the party at Blossom's. I had already despatched Mrs. Tate to the cinema, insisting that she just *had* to watch a film I had recommended. I didn't want her to be in any danger.

'Sure you'll be all right, Rebecca?' he asked.

I smiled: 'I hope so, Gil. But there's no other way. It *has* to be done like this. You know what to do?'

He nodded: 'Yes. I am to keep constant watch, and when the killer goes out, I'll be following, out of sight.'

He reached into his jacket. 'Here's my spare gun for your additional protection.'

Gil pulled out a revolver and a handful of bullets, which he carefully inserted.

'Just in case . . . ' and he handed me the loaded weapon. 'Just point and pull the trigger. You can't miss.'

By the time I had hidden the weapon under my settee cushion, he had gone, leaving me seated on the settee. I picked up the self-help book on modeling, and began reading.

I glanced at the watch on my wrist, and noted with surprise that only half an hour had passed since his departure. I wasn't really reading at all — I glanced at the pages, but my mind was dancing with fear and determination, courage and cowardice.

Well, I was ready, and although there might be great danger, it wasn't anything to what I would have done for Mike. Mike, shut away behind cold walls, imprisoned for a crime he hadn't had anything to do with, and with guilt so firmly fixed on him that he was almost certain to be electrocuted if my plan failed!

It mustn't fail! Nothing must go wrong!

I sat on, glancing through the pages, keyed up; every now and again my eyes flitted involuntarily to the door. It was unlocked.

Time dragged by . . . I judged that over at Blossom's the party must now be well under way.

There was a soft tap at the door, and it began to open . . . slowly . . .

I sat up, still holding the book. If this was my party I had to be careful to do nothing which might cause alarm and abandonment of the planned attack on me. I had to act as though I was surprised.

Blossom Pennant stepped into the room!

So I had been right. Her unusually deep voice had been mistaken for that of a man by the police when she had telephoned to frame Mike.

'There you are, my dear,' she said, smiling. 'So you *did* stay in after all?'

'Why, Blossom, what brings you over here, away from your guests?' I asked her, raising my eyebrows.

She slumped into a chair and lit a cigarette. She said: 'They won't miss me. Fortunately. That's the best of my parties — the fools get so drunk they couldn't even keep an eye on their own shadows, you know. I thought I'd slip along and try to cheer you up about Mike . . . '

I shook my head. 'That's impossible. As long as they're holding him for something he didn't do . . . '

She wasn't listening; she had removed her monocle and was polishing it with her handkerchief. She said: 'It really was stupid of you to pose for Gil — in view of what happened to his *other* models. What made you do it, my dear?'

'I needed money. I have to live.'

'But you have condemned yourself to *death*,' she told me.

I tensed. 'I don't understand you, Blossom.'

'You don't? Look what happened to the *others* . . . '

Her eyes were suddenly gazing at me; they were sharp and glowing. Her supple hands lay in her lap, but her fingers were moving slowly and sinuously, like tiny serpents.

She went on: 'They all died! All died horribly. Why should you be the exception?'

I sat staring at her eyes; they fascinated me. My hand went to my throat. I said: 'You — you *killed them*!'

A queer smile crossed her features; the moustache on her upper lip seemed ridiculous, incongruous, as did the monocle. The eyes glittered with strange fires, shifting pin points of maniacal light. The pupils were dilated . . . her hands writhed on her knees.

'Yes, my dear. I killed them. I hated them — hated them for what they had meant to Gil, for the beauty he had seen in them, beauty that he failed to see in me! I hated them for their loose morals, their conscious knowledge of their own beauty and their knowledge of my complete ugliness. My curse! Ugly, manlike, with no pretensions to being anything any man could ever want. All my life it's been like that; all my life I've been a hanger-on, an unwanted member of the set here, tolerated because of my money, despised because of my lack of artistic ability, abhorred because of my ugliness. It didn't much matter then; then there was no one. Men were insignificant to me, nor had I ever felt any regard for any of them. I was strong enough to be self-sufficient, to get along without men. I worked hard to turn out good art, painted day and night, spent hundreds on lessons, equipment, models, studios . . .

'Nothing helped. The fact always remained that as an artist I was — hopeless — and at last it began to be borne in on me that I never had turned out any worthwhile work, and never would! It was at that time that Gil first settled down in the district. He was introduced to me through a friend, and he liked to come round and talk to me. No, he didn't see anything in me. He treated me as a man, as a companion, but nothing else. He liked to talk things over with me. We had both travelled a great deal, and could discuss the little places we remembered, the beauty of things and places we had seen . . .

'He borrowed a large sum of money from me. He could have taken my entire fortune, merely for the asking. He could have taken anything I owned or hoped to own.

'For I — yes, I, Blossom Pennant, ugly, withered, hopeless, almost unnatural — had fallen in love with *him*! And if I

227

had never loved before, I loved with three times the intensity of an ordinary love! I worshipped him, believed in him and his work, and I was fool enough to hope he might love *me*! That which I could not offer him in physical attraction could be replaced by mental pleasures — how wrong I was!

'I remember when I casually suggested he should stay the night once, the look of detestation he gave me. For the first time he saw I was a woman, with a woman's desires. I don't think he realized the extent of my affection for him. He thought it was simply that he had happened to be on the spot, that any man would have fulfilled the need.

'He came less and less after that time, and I knew he was trying to drop me off gradually. By my lack of control I had turned him away from even the mental attractions I offered him.

'Then his work began to sell. He took a larger studio, hired models, took time over his paintings. I saw him no more!

'I took to throwing parties for the younger set. He would come to those, not

228

because he liked them, but because the memory of the money I had once lent him troubled his conscience, and also because he knew he could talk to me, enjoy an intelligent chat, without being embarrassed by any suggestions I might forward.

'How I loathed and hated those parties and the type of people who attended them! Silly, gibbering, sexually-depraved clowns! Women without a shred of decency or respect, and with no regard for their bodies — those bodies I would have given my fortune for, could I but have exchanged them for this dry, withered frame of mine! Those bodies that Gil painted, that attracted him and won his admiration!'

I was listening fascinatedly; her eyes were burning with a fire of hate as she relived her memories. Her hands were still.

She continued: 'It went on like that until Gil's first painting was finished. The woman who posed for him had the face of an angel, the mind of a harlot. I scorned her, but Gil — despite her mental negligibility — worshiped her. He could see only the *outward* beauty. That there was corruption and filth within he knew not, and cared not.

'And one night she called on me. She called on me to tell me that when she and Gil were married she meant to get him away from Greenwich Village, to take him somewhere where she could live the life of a lady. She as good as told me that his money was the principal attraction — she thought he would go far.

'I was insane enough to warn her that I would tell Gil what she planned, and something about me must have told her the mad truth! She laughed uproariously and taxed me with being in love with Gil. She said she would shout it out all over the Village, make me the idiotic laughing stock of every man and woman I knew. She pointed out my defects — I saw red suddenly. My control snapped, and I threw myself at her; gripped her by the throat.

'It was done. I took the corpse out down the fire-escape, carried it through the shadows threw it into a nearby garbage can. Then I went home.'

She paused and smiled: 'I was never suspected. *Never*. How simple it was; how *easy*! I committed three of the murders whilst I was holding parties. Ostensibly I would go into the kitchen to cut sandwiches. Then I would sneak out by way of the fire-escape by the kitchen window, and back the same way. I destroyed all the girls who posed for him! Destroyed that beauty he had admired, that beauty I could never have! Killed them — because the first one had shown me how easy it was to do so — and because I begrudged them the time they had spent in his company, hated the admiration which impelled him to convey their forms to his canvas, and felt angry at the way his work held him away from me.

'Yes, it was I who was foolish enough to leave that cigarette in Mornia's rooms. It was I who hurried to Marcia's and later phoned the police, so that they could apprehend Mike. They assumed the voice was a man's; mine is rather deep. That explains it. They assumed the strength required to do the killings must have meant the strangler was a man. They

231

overlooked the fact that *I* am the next thing to a man — and fully as strong as *any* man in *this* district!'

I whispered: 'Why — why did you try to pin the murders on Mike? Do you bear him any ill-will?'

'I feel neither one way nor the other about your friend Mike, but I was aware you were posing for Gil. I knew you must be my next victim once Marcia was put out the way. Therefore I was able to arrange that Mike should not be here to protect you. I wanted you alone — as you are *now*!'

'And — the paintings — the ones you bought from Gil?'

'I destroyed them,' she said savagely. 'Slashed them to *ribbons*. Destroyed all that remained of Gil's admirations! As I will destroy *yours* when I have it — as I will destroy *you*!'

She rose suddenly. I shrank back on the settee. She made claws of her hands. Her face worked strangely. Her eyes held me trembling and weak in my place. She came slowly towards me, hands outstretched.

'*Help!*' I screamed. 'Gil — you can come in now!'

She said: 'Gil is at the party, and the house is quite deserted. I made sure of that. No one can hear you!'

Then her fingers were at my throat, were digging deep, cutting off my breath, destroying my life!

Flecks of foam were on her lips; her face was warped and contorted with her insanity, and there was no sign of Gil! I felt myself getting weaker as I struggled to throw her off, to tear away her grip from my neck, to squirm free. It was a useless struggle. For she held me with an iron grip, her knee dug deep into my stomach, her full weight forcing me down onto the settee.

I had not wanted to make use of the revolver which I had prepared and hidden beneath the cushion I was on, but now I knew there was no other way out. Dizzy and reeling, I groped downwards, felt my fingers close about the butt.

I pulled the revolver up, forced my hand between us and screwed the gun round until it pointed at her chest.

I pulled the trigger!

The shots rang out clear and sharp, three of them. Blossom's face stopped working suddenly, her hands went slack. As she fell backwards away from me, the monocle slid from her eye, where it had stayed firmly all through the struggle, and dropped on the floor.

She thudded down between chair and settee, and hardly had she fallen than the door flew open and Gil rushed in, gun in hand. He gasped with relief when he saw me, panted: 'You're all right? *Thank God!* She slipped out by way of the back kitchen window. I only just found out . . . has she been here?'

I pointed to the space before me, and he came round and stared down . . . there was a crunching sound; he moved aside, and where his foot had fallen the shattered fragments of Blossom's monocle were revealed . . .

*　*　*

We telephoned for the police, and officers arrived, along with medics who rushed

Blossom to hospital. Gil and I were taken back to the police precinct, where we were closely questioned by an apoplectic inspector. It was only after we had signed the statement he prepared that we were allowed to return home, well into the early hours. Nor was I allowed to see Mike until the following evening, when he was officially released from custody, and came to my rooms. The police had only just allowed me to return to them, and I'd had to spend the night with the shocked Mrs. Tate, who had returned from the cinema whilst we were at the precinct, to find us gone and her property swarming with police. The police had allowed me to pen her an explanatory note, which an officer had handed to her. Even so, the poor dear had almost passed out with shock, she told me.

'So that's all there was to it, Mike,' I told him, nestling close. 'They took her to hospital, and she died soon after giving a confession. In one way I feel sorry for her . . . '

Mike said: 'And you risked all that for me?'

'I'd do it over again, Mike, any time.'

'You know,' he said, thinking, 'when this gets out, the newspapers will be clamoring for your story. You can make a small fortune telling it!'

I smiled. 'I'd never thought of that . . . '

'It means,' Mike went on, 'that you can maybe find a decent place for your family to live, help your sisters get a good start in life.'

Before I could say anything more, he closed my lips with his own and held me closely. The door opened and Gil looked in, said: 'I thought I'd bring you two my engagement present now. It isn't much, but I thought you might like it.'

He slid the painting he had done of me inside the door with a smile.

THE END

We do hope that you have enjoyed reading this large print book.

Did you know that all of our titles are available for purchase?

We publish a wide range of high quality large print books including:
Romances, Mysteries, Classics
General Fiction
Non Fiction and Westerns

Special interest titles available in large print are:
The Little Oxford Dictionary
Music Book, Song Book
Hymn Book, Service Book

Also available from us courtesy of Oxford University Press:
Young Readers' Dictionary
(large print edition)
Young Readers' Thesaurus
(large print edition)

For further information or a free brochure, please contact us at:
Ulverscroft Large Print Books Ltd.,
The Green, Bradgate Road, Anstey,
Leicester, LE7 7FU, England.
Tel: (00 44) 0116 236 4325
Fax: (00 44) 0116 234 0205

Other titles in the
Linford Mystery Library:

BLOOD MONEY

Catriona McCuaig

1948. Midwife Maudie Rouse looks forward to working with Llandyfan's handsome new doctor, Leonard Lennox, but is he all that he seems? When a young woman named Paula Mason turns up claiming to be his fiancée, this sets into motion a train of events that leads to her murder. The doctor is arrested, but the facts don't add up, and Maudie is determined to investigate. But could she be in danger of being murdered herself?

THE HOUSE OF THE GOAT

Gerald Verner

Investigating the murder of a shabby man who had asked directions to the home of Lord Lancroft before being found brutally stabbed, Superintendent Budd has only one clue. Inside the man's jacket is a piece of paper, on which is written the Lord's name and address, and the words 'The House of the Goat' . . . And when an ancient mummy is stolen in the search for a mysterious ring, nothing is as it seems . . .

CODE OF SILENCE

Arlette Lees

When Sterling Seabright is found strangled in the woods outside the small farming community of Abundance, Wisconsin, even her closest friends are shocked to learn of her secret life. When a second body is found murdered in a cabin by the lake, it's up to Deputies Robely Danner and Frack Tilsley to discover the link. Sterling's classmates hold various pieces of the puzzle, and although they may be talking among themselves, Robely and Frack are unable to break their code of silence . . .

ZONE ZERO

John Robb

Western powers plan to explode a hydrogen bomb in a remote area of Southern Algeria — code named Zone Zero. The zone has to be evacuated. Fort Ney is the smallest Foreign Legion outpost in the zone, commanded by a young lieutenant. Here, too, is the English legionnaire, tortured by previous cowardice, as well as a little Greek who has within him the spark of greatness. It has always been a peaceful place — until the twelve travellers arrive. Now the outwitted garrison faces the uttermost limit of horror . . .

THE WEIRD SHADOW OVER MORECAMBE

Edmund Glasby

Professor Mandrake Smith would be unrecognisable to his former colleagues now: the shambling, drink-addled erstwhile Professor of Anthropology at Oxford is now barely surviving in Morecambe. He has many things to forget, although some don't want to forget him. Plagued by nightmares from his past, both in Oxford and Papua New Guinea, he finds himself drafted by the enigmatic Mr. Thorn, whom he grudgingly assists in trying to stop the downward spiral into darkness and insanity that awaits Morecambe — and the entire world . . .